ROUNDED IN DREAM

Paul Marsh

MINERVA PRESS
LONDON
ATLANTA MONTREUX SYDNEY

ROUNDED IN DREAM

ISBN 0 75410 480 X

First Published 1998 by
MINERVA PRESS
195 Knightsbridge
London SW7 1RE

Printed in Great Britain for Minerva Press

ROUNDED IN DREAM

Despite some place names being unchanged and locations described as they existed at the time of this story, all the events in this book are fictional, and the characters entirely imaginary.

S'en vendra en brief temps meschié
Sus celz qui nous dampnent a tort:
Diex en vengera nostre mort.

Seignors, dist il, sachiez, sanz tere,
Que touz celz qui nous sont contrere
Por nous en aront a souffrir.

♦

Let evil swiftly befall
Those who have wrongly condemned us;
God will avenge our death.

Sirs, he said, know, without any doubt,
That all those who are against us
For us will suffer.

An extract from an anonymous verse account in
Old French of Jacques de Molay's curse. It is commonly
attributed to Geoffroi de Paris, a royal clerk.

Sources

The author wishes to acknowledge the following three works for their invaluable information concerning the Knights Templar, the dissolution of the Order and the execution of Grand Master Jacques de Molay and Geoffroi de Charney, Preceptor of Normandy:

Burman, Edward, *Supremely Abominable Crimes: The Trial of the Knights Templar*, London, Allison and Busby, 1994.

Robinson, John J., *Dungeon, Fire and Sword: The Knights Templar In the Crusades,* London, Michael O'Mara Books Ltd, 1994.

Seward, Desmond, *The Monks of War: The Military Religious Orders,* London, Penguin, 1995.

Geoffroi de Paris's verse account of the de Molay curse (the original in Old French and the translation) quoted in the epigraph, is derived from the Burman work, where it appears in a more complete form. It is reprinted here by permission of Allison and Busby Ltd.

Floor plan of Bangalore

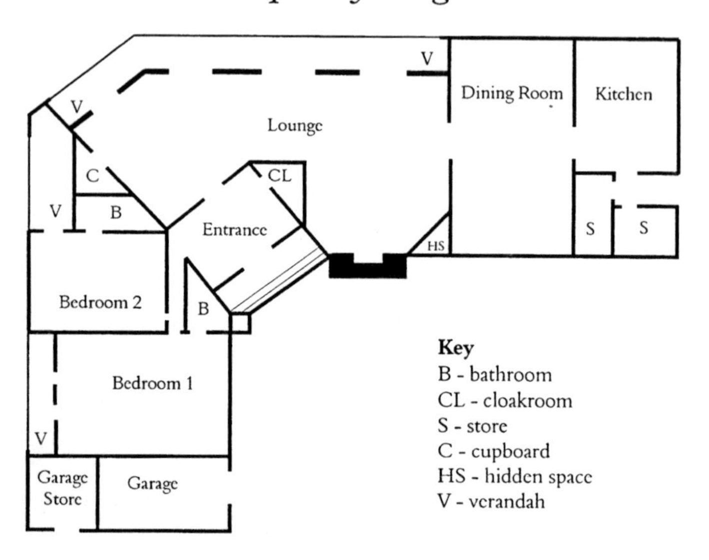

Site plan

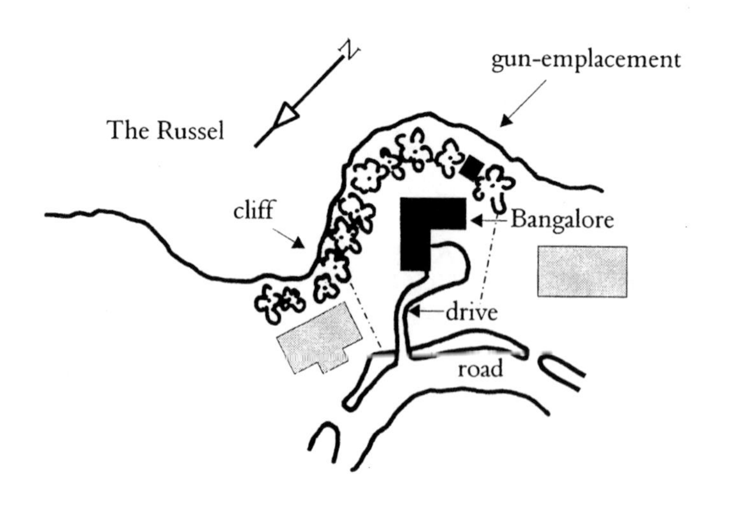

Prologue

Known by the French as *les îles Anglo-Normandes* or *les îles de la Manche*, by the British as simply the Channel Islands, these tiny scraps of land off the west coast of the Cherbourg peninsula are places of legend and mystery. They are too small to fight over (although the Nazis considered them worthy of occupation during the Second World War) and so they have continued in a strangely equivocal situation for little short of a thousand years – the last lands of the ancient dukedom of Normandy to remain in British ownership.

When William the Conqueror set up court in Britain in 1066, the Channel Islands were a small part of his existing domain. They became, therefore, a British possession and thus have remained to this day – a part of Britain, yet hardly British; islands with a proud sense of independence and a people who considers itself in every way superior to its mainland neighbour and, as such, never wholly subjected to British mainland law and practice. This people still clings to many ancient, pre-British rites and traditions – as it does to its myths and fantasies.

Strange things have happened on these islands, often never recorded, but passed by word of mouth from generation to generation – happenings that are only talked about in whispers – strange, sinister events whose tendrils thrust deep into the affairs of both France and Britain. The islanders, the genuine islanders whose family trees have been rooted for centuries in the parishes of the islands, have a fierce individuality, proud of their independence, their isolation, their relationship with the sea and their historic links with mainland France. Only since the Second World War have things started to change, but the Channel Islands have remained special, jealously guarding their mysteries. This was the state of play at the time when the events of this story took place, some ten years after the end of the Occupation.

As far as the geography of the Channel Islands is concerned, there are three major islands; Alderney, the smallest of the three and the one furthest to the north, yet closest to the coast of France; Jersey, the largest and most southerly of the group; and Guernsey, the location of the main happenings in this tale, lying roughly midway between the other two islands. Guernsey is the second largest Channel Island (but still only a mere fifty thousand hectares in size) and is mother hen to a posse of island chicks – the tiny excrescences of Sark, Herm and Jetou, divided from Guernsey's eastern shore by a narrow strip of water, The Russel.

To these islands came (and still come) the rich and retiring, eager to take advantage of the benefits of a benign tax regime. In the summer the holidaymakers arrive, attracted by the climate, cheap booze and tobacco, and – in the 1950s before 'going abroad' had caught on – the thrill of almost being abroad, but not quite. These summer visitors rarely break the surface of the secret islands. They skate through their sunshine fortnight with an almost perpetual hangover, sorely sunburnt shoulders and the feeling – correct, as it turns out – that the locals dislike them, but are prepared to take their money. The rich and retiring, on the other hand, create their own tier of society, their own ghetto, comprising only their own kind and ignoring, as far as possible, the real society that surrounds it. This real society consists of a traditional people, steeped in mystery and legend of other times, when these tiny scraps of land were much more neatly ravelled into the affairs of the world.

Only sometimes – on rare occasions and to very special people – the weft of reality bulges to allow near-forgotten fact and fantasy to leak through into a dreaming human brain, giving proof of the realism that crouches behind the legend. Just such an unexpected revelation happened to Jennie James, returning to the islands after an absence of many years.

It is one example of an untold number of stories, mostly unrecorded and rarely important in the affairs of man. In this respect, the story of Jennie James is different. In her case the weft of time gaped wide enough to allow her sleeping mind to acquire an accurate insight into past happenings, which were about to influence the life around her, with horrific consequences.

Chapter One

It was during the dying years of the 1950s that Jennie James came to Guernsey in search of a fresh beginning and a new home in which to hide from a life that had treated her unkindly. Almost immediately she stumbled upon Bangalore, a bungalow of character, set on the cliff top to the south of the island's main town, St Peter Port. With that discovery she triggered off a sequence of events which was to lead her down many mysterious and ancient byways.

Bangalore was an eccentric property; not threateningly eccentric, merely idiosyncratic in a homely sort of way. This, as far as Jennie was concerned, added to its charm and its undoubted quality of uniqueness. Of course its setting was superb, with views over The Russel to the minor Channel Islands of Sark, Herm and Jetou.

The bungalow's chief eccentricity was its plan. Designed in the form of a letter 'L', so as to allow all its major rooms the benefit of the magnificent sea views, its architect had thrust its spacious entrance hall – extravagantly oversized for a 1930s bungalow – obliquely into the angle at the meeting of the two arms of the L, plunging walls at unexpected angles into the rooms on either side. This cavalier disregard for the right angle resulted in quaintly shaped rooms, which were inappropriate to formal furniture layouts, but ideal for the creation of little 'nests' scattered about the sprawling lounge area. After her first visit to the property, Jennie described this unusual characteristic of the house to her friends on the mainland as having 'rooms with corners missing.'

But Bangalore's eccentricities did not end with the shapes of its rooms. It had its own peculiar sound which murmured a continuous counterpoint to all the more usual noises of an inhabited building. Even on windless nights, Bangalore moaned and sighed, not disconcertingly so, but somehow agreeably, as though to emphasise its essential 'homeliness' – another of Jennie's descriptions of the place. She was to speculate many times during her life there, what the source of this sound was, but could never quite make up her mind. It probably arose from a combination of noises, she thought – the distant growling of the sea against the cliffs at the end of Bangalore's garden, the wind stirring the branches of the conifer trees that lined the top of the cliff and the raceway for breezes, created by the verandahs – some open, some enclosed – which graced the two façades of the bungalow facing the sea.

These verandahs had been incorporated into the design at the request of Bangalore's original owner. They, together with the property's name, acted as permanent reminders of the gin-swilling colonial career from which he had retired to take up residence on the Channel Islands. Jennie could imagine him, on summer evenings, sitting in a wicker wing chair on the lounge verandah, trying in vain to recapture those exciting days, when half the map of the world was coloured red.

Jennie was fascinated by Bangalore. If ever there was a case of love at first sight, this was it. In some strange way it was as though she already knew the place, recognised its nooks and crannies, had already luxuriated in its warmth on a frosty winter's night, its coolness on a sultry, bee-laden midsummer eve. Yet this was no common *déjà-vu* experience. It was more a comfortable feeling of meeting a well-known friend after years of separation.

'It's delightful – just what I'm looking for,' she admitted to the old lady, the present owner, who showed her around when she went to view the property, '– the house and, particularly, the garden.'

'Yes, it is delightful, isn't it?' The old woman smiled ingenuously at Jennie. 'We had to leave it during the war, of course – that nearly broke our hearts – and when we came back, so much needed doing. The place was in a such a state – so much to put right. It really upset poor Charles; but he set to work and got it finished – all done, just in time.'

Just in time for what was not made clear, and Jennie thought it seemed somehow impertinent to pursue the matter, although she didn't know why. Instead she merely said, 'You must hate leaving it now.'

The old woman shrugged her shoulders. 'There comes a time to move on,' was her only reply.

Suddenly Jennie was overcome by a feeling of dejection. 'It really is lovely, but I'm sure I couldn't possibly afford it.'

'My dear; you go and talk to my agents about it. I'm a fool where figures are concerned and they – the agents, I mean – have full authority to negotiate. Go and talk to them. I'm sure you won't be wasting your time.'

Jennie was struck by the similarity of the old woman's words to those of Mr Johnson at the estate agent's, when she had pointed out to him that there was no asking price on his company's information sheet about Bangalore.

Placing his elbows on his desk, finger tips meeting in front of his chin, he had said, 'It is a specific requirement of the vendor – no talk about money until the prospective purchaser has viewed the property. But, believe me, Mrs James, you will not be wasting your time if you view Bangalore. It is a quite exceptional property and Mrs Grace the original owner's widow – is such a fine lady. I'll arrange an appointment, shall I? You won't be disappointed, I can assure you.'

And so it had come about that on a sweet-scented spring morning with daffodils peppering the grass under the conifers at the edge of Bangalore's spacious garden, Jennie James had paid Mrs Grace a visit. She, indeed, had not been disappointed by what she saw; although she was disturbed by the fear that she would not be able to afford the asking price. After viewing what she had come to think of as the ideal property, it would be a bitter disappointment to find it beyond her pocket. Bangalore was just what she wanted – not too big – quite compact really, but with a spacious wrap-around lounge with fantastic views over the sea. Other features included two bedrooms (she had no plans to receive many visitors at one time) and a beautifully fitted kitchen. She felt the house would be easy to run, was not overlooked by its neighbours and had a fine, well-kept garden – tidy flower beds near the house and wide lawns, fading to rough-mown grass under the conifers that formed a wind break along the cliff top.

But why the coyness over the price?

Once more Jennie found herself sitting in front of Mr Johnson's desk, her heart pounding with, what seemed to her, unnecessary vigour. It was almost like being a girl again, she thought to herself, waiting outside the head's study for examination results.

'Ah, Mrs James; you liked Bangalore then?' Mr Johnson's eyes twinkled behind his glasses. 'I suspect you did. You could hardly fail to, could you?'

'Oh yes; I liked Bangalore very much indeed,' she replied. 'But what about the price? I'm sure I won't be able to afford it. My means, as I explained to you before, are limited.'

'The asking price is...' and Mr Johnson named a figure just comfortably within Jennie's upper limit.

'Really,' she exclaimed. 'I can't believe it; particularly bearing in mind the way property prices on the island seem to have rocketed since the war.'

'I did tell you, you would not be wasting your time, Mrs James. You should have trusted me. The reason is very simple really. You see Mrs Grace has little need of the money. She has no children and Mr Grace left her well provided for. I fancy there are other factors than mere money influencing this sale. A fellow feeling for another widowed lady, maybe.'

Johnson's eyes continued to sparkle behind his glasses. He seemed quite a nice old chap, thought Jennie, much more human than he appeared at first sight. For all of ten seconds she hesitated. Whilst she had no desire to feel the recipient of charity from anyone, she wanted Bangalore so fervently that she cared little for Mrs Grace's motives. Without further delay she instructed Mr Johnson to inform his client that she had a purchaser.

*

Jennie's delight with the prospect of living in Bangalore was expressed in a series of excited telephone calls to her friends on the mainland. Chief among these was John Frensham. It was he who had remained firmly supportive during the long months of depression she had suffered after her bereavement. In this way he had earned a special place in Jennie's affections – a real friend, yet in some ways more than a friend. It was he whom she told first.

'Oh, John, I just can't believe my good fortune,' she had said. 'Immediately I saw the place, I knew this was where my future lay. I've never felt like this about any other property. Bangalore is sheer heaven. Finding it was an incredible piece of luck. It must have been preordained.'

John Frensham listened to her excited babble without enthusiasm – and as he did so, he could feel his own hopes for the future evaporating. He found it impossible to reciprocate her delight. Glumly he congratulated her on her good fortune, listened to her promise to keep in touch and hung up.

And that was how Jennie James linked her life to the past, present and future of a bungalow called Bangalore on the Channel Island of Guernsey, and thereby started an affair that would last until both she and it ran out of time.

Meanwhile, across the Channel in Guildford, John Frensham skilfully poured a bottle of Double Diamond into a glass, tilting it at just the right angle and pouring 'over his thumb', as his father had taught him, so as not to fill the glass with froth, drank it in a couple of long draughts and sadly reviewed his shattered dreams. 'I only hope the woman knows what she's doing,' he muttered, and toasted things that could never be.

⋆

Some days afterwards, when the formalities of the purchase were well underway, Jennie tried to ring Mrs Grace to make a date when she could visit Bangalore again, this time to take a closer look at one or two features of the property and, maybe, note down a few measurements for carpets and curtains. She heard the ringing tone repeated endlessly, but there was no reply. She tried again several times during that day and the next, but still there was no response.

Time after time during the next week Jennie redialled the number, but still no one answered. At length she sought the help of Mr Johnson. He sounded surprised.

'Oh, but Mrs Grace has left the island,' he explained. 'Did she not tell you? It is unlikely that she'll return, I should think.'

'Gone? So quickly?' Jennie exclaimed. 'How unexpected!'

'Yes, she left almost immediately after accepting your offer,' he told her. 'She was only staying on in Bangalore until the right purchaser could be found. Evidently things awaited her on the mainland, I understand. I doubt whether we shall see Mrs Grace again on Guernsey. It is a pity. She is a wonderful lady – and did so much good work for the community. But I suppose the island held too many memories for her.'

Having recently suffered the death of a loved one, Jennie could understand and was full of sympathy. 'How long ago was it that Mr Grace died?' she asked. Mr Johnson's reply thrust an unexpected chill into her heart.

'Oh, quite a few years ago, I think. He died on the mainland, I believe. Latterly we never saw very much of him here. He was never so active in the community as Mrs Grace.'

'But surely Bangalore hasn't been on the market for several years?'

Mr Johnson laughed. 'Oh no, dear lady. Hardly would such a desirable property at such an attractive price have remained long on the market. Your timing, if I may say so, Mrs James, was most fortuitous. Mrs Grace had only just decided to sell when you approached us with your requirements.' His words skilfully avoided answering the questions that were flying around in Jennie's head. Why, after several years of widowhood, had Mrs Grace suddenly decided to sell? And then to depart from the island with such haste!

Jennie found the whole thing incredible. She recalled Mrs Grace's words, 'There comes a time to move on.' But to leave a place she obviously loved so much. And to go so precipitately too. Surely she had given Jennie the impression that Charles Grace had been involved in the renovations of Bangalore after the Occupation. Yet Mr Johnson had suggested that he had not been very much on the island since the war.

How strange, thought Jennie, but soon the mystery was forgotten in the excitement of arranging her removal into her new home. Everything went like clockwork. The formalities were executed with remarkable speed and within a few weeks Jennie was presented with the keys of Bangalore – the eccentric bungalow in which the improbable always seemed about to happen. This aptitude for producing the unexpected was illustrated even on the first day Jennie had the keys.

She had decided to move in straight away. 'I shall camp out,' she had told her friend, John Frensham, in another phone call. 'Move in as soon as I get the keys and make do with things, like carpets and curtains. There's no need to rush with final arrangements. I'll get my bits and pieces delivered from the mainland and make do with them, until I've had a chance to think. Getting in is the important thing. Once I'm settled in my dream house, I can spend time getting things just the way I want them.' And so it was that the day before the removal firm was scheduled to arrive with Jennie's 'bits and pieces', she paid her second visit to Bangalore.

*

As she had expected, everything in the bungalow was in accordance with the terms of the sale. Her brief experience of Mrs Grace had encouraged her to have no forebodings on that score. In addition, the property had been left immaculately clean after the old lady's effects had been removed. A shock, however, awaited Jennie in the main bedroom.

There, in the otherwise bare room, stood a truly magnificent, antique double bed. It was clearly of oriental origin and was in superb condition. Its mahogany head and foot boards were heavily carved and within the similarly carved edge boards lay an apparently new mattress. Jennie stood for a moment at the bedroom door quite disconcerted by the unexpectedness (not to mention, the sheer beauty) of the bed.

Slowly, as though hardly daring to move for fear of breaking a dream, she crept into the room and approached the bed. She stole around it, admiring its carving, fingering its deeply undercut motifs and stroking the satin-smooth surface of the wood, matured by years of waxing. Finally, somewhat breathlessly, she sat on the mattress – and immediately knew that this would be the most comfortable bed on which she had ever slept. She kicked off her shoes and lay full-length on the mattress. It gave under her weight, firm, but yielding. And then she saw the note. It was pinned to the mattress – a scrap of paper, on which was written in a tiny, but legible, hand:

Dear Mrs James,

This dear bed is so much a part of Bangalore, I hadn't the heart to take it away. Please accept it with my best wishes for a happy life in Bangalore – in what has always been a very special place for my husband and I. If you use the bed, I am confident that you will enjoy sound, deep and satisfying sleep – of that I have no doubt. My husband loved this bed, almost as much as he loved Bangalore. You now have his two most cherished possessions.

The note was signed 'Sarah Grace'. There was a postscript too: *The mattress is nearly new and, as you can see, very clean.*

'Well how extraordinary!' Jennie cried. 'And yet how kind – how very kind.'

She got up from the bed and moved thoughtfully about the room. Despite her delight, there was something troubling about the gift. To leave behind two of her husband's most cherished possessions – one of which was so eminently movable – seemed extremely odd. In her mind, Jennie was comparing Mrs Grace's action with her own insistence on keeping all her husband's pictures, even the ones which were, to her taste, unlovely.

There was another uncanny feature of the bed, and one which only became obvious after the removal team had positioned Jennie's other pieces of bedroom furniture – dressing table, wardrobes and bedside cabinets – alongside Mrs Grace's 'dear bed'. Only then was it apparent that it was not the least bit incongruous with Jennie's more modern furniture. On the contrary, the two styles complemented each other tastefully.

'It shall stay,' Jennie decided. 'Mrs Grace's "dear bed" shall not have a new home. It shall stay just where she left it. It was such a kind thought. I really must thank her.'

Once more she sought the help of Mr Johnson. On the phone his voice sounded puzzled. 'Mrs Grace's address on the mainland? Oh I really couldn't say.' And then a note of concern crept in. 'I trust there is no problem. Everything is all right at Bangalore, I hope, Mrs James.'

'Yes, quite all right – in fact more than all right. Mrs Grace has done some really rather charming things – some surprises for my moving in, you might say – and I wanted to write and thank her.'

'Ah, yes; Mrs Grace is a fine lady. Unfortunately all our dealings with her since she left the island pass through her solicitors, Grumely and Creech. Maybe you could send your letter to her, care of them.'

And that was precisely what Jennie did. Though whether Mrs Grace ever received her letter, she was never to know, as there was no acknowledgement.

★

Jennie's first night at Bangalore was still and moonlit. As with all first experiences of new homes, there was about it an air of unreality, enhanced, no doubt, by the Bangalore sound which quickly lulled Jennie to sleep in Mrs Grace's magnificent bed. Her rest, however, though deep, was not entirely adventure-free. Towards dawn one dream came to her, so vivid that it left a clear impression of every detail in her memory when she awoke.

It was night-time. She was standing on the moonlit lawn of Bangalore, listening to the sounds of the sea against the cliffs. The air was heavy with the perfume of night-scented stocks. Suddenly a tall man, not young, yet sprightly and erect, stepped out of the trees on the cliff top and walked deliberately across the lawn towards the house. As he approached the steps up to the verandah on the bedroom wing, he turned towards Jennie, smiled and waved an ingenuous and friendly greeting. Then he mounted the steps and disappeared inside the house. His manner was of someone returning home after an evening stroll, relaxed and at peace with his surroundings. What was more, Jennie felt no threat from his presence, just a quiet contentment.

Strangely she had almost believed that she recognised the man, as he walked across the lawn. There was something familiar about his loose-limbed stride, the hunch of his shoulders, the way he held his head – and yet how could there be?

Awake once more, Jennie lay for some time in the comfortable bed, trying unsuccessfully to analyse the curiously equivocal impression with which her first sighting of the stranger had left her. In succeeding days and weeks she would renew this acquaintance and continue her struggle to understand, but it would be many months before there would be even a partial solution to her uncertainty.

Chapter Two

After the excited flurry of telephone calls from Jennie before she moved into Bangalore, John Frensham heard nothing of her activities on Guernsey for some time. Then, about a month after she had taken up residence, a letter fell on to his doormat that was addressed in, what had become for him, a very familiar hand.

It had occurred to him that he might have upset her by his failure to disguise his lack of enthusiasm, when she broke the news of her purchase of Bangalore. 'I only hope you know what you're doing. Are you sure it's the right thing for you?' These were the sort of remarks that came tumbling out, in spite of the dampening effect he knew they would have. But he could not avoid speaking his mind. He was aware of a desperate feeling of unease at what his friend was doing. How could he have shared her joy, as he stood bleakly in his lonely hallway, listening to the enthusiastic chatter on the other end of the line? How else could he have reacted, when all he could think about was Jennie's vulnerability, and his desire to provide her with the shield from life's cruelty that he believed she badly needed since Greg had died?

From their school days, Jennie's late husband, Greg, and he had been close friends. After Greg's sudden death, John, himself by then a widower, had helped Jennie sort out the inevitable muddle that such unexpected events bring in their wake. Afterwards he had continued to keep a watchful, but non-intrusive, eye on her struggle with newly experienced loneliness. He was not a demonstrative man and did not believe in thrusting himself upon others, unless he was sure his attentions were required. And so he had stood in the background, his true interest possibly never recognised by its object.

For two years Jennie had remained in the house in Guildford, where she and Greg had lived for fifteen years in tolerable harmony. It had not been a bad marriage, although by no means free from turbulence in its early years. No children had ever resulted from their lovemaking, although Jennie had urgently desired them. Then, just as maturity was about to take control of their relationship, Greg had died – at work, sitting at his desk one Friday morning. There had been no previous warning that his heart would one day prematurely fail him. Jennie had been stupefied by the shock and for many weeks afterwards remained palely desolate. John had watched over her, making sure she was coping with all those prosaic affairs which have to be attended to at such times and which prove so tiresome – watching and waiting, whilst she picked up the pieces of her shattered life.

Indeed, he had grown very fond of her and began to nurse a hope that one day, maybe, their relationship might become more close. They got on well together, had similar interests, laughed at the same jokes and lost their tempers over similar injustices. When Jennie first broke the news to John that she was going to sell up and move back to her birthplace in the Channel Islands, he was astounded. Nothing had prepared him for this. Suddenly his world lost a substantial part of its interest. It was not dissimilar, he mused, to his feelings when his own wife had died, a few years before – a feeling that there was no longer any point to his life, if it had to be lived alone. For a time he puzzled over the strength of this sensation. He had not realised how much Jennie had grown to mean to him. And now here she was, about to slip through his fingers. Should he have made a move earlier – an attempt to express his feelings for her in words? Then he became absorbed in the impossible task of trying to understand her motives for such a move – trying to find some rational explanation for her decision. She was still young, in her early forties. Why should she not start a new life in totally new surroundings? But still he found her impulse to cast herself off in this way – from himself and her other mainland friends – hard to understand.

However much he tried to tell himself that maybe this move was best for Jennie, his own bleak disappointment was irreconcilable. Why Guernsey? Why so far away? She had not lived there since she was a child and, as far as he knew, none of her relatives still remained on the island. And so it had been that with a sinking heart he had offered to drive her down to Southampton on the day she was scheduled to leave on the Channel Islands ferry.

'I do hope you're making the right decision,' he had told her. 'Don't jump into anything too quickly, anything that'll tie you down – property, that sort of thing – until you're quite certain Guernsey is the place for you. Give yourself time. Take a good look around before you commit yourself to anything.'

'You know me, John,' she had replied, 'always cautious.' In her mind were memories of her response to John's agonised attempt at the eleventh hour to persuade her to marry him and stay in Guildford.

He, too, thought of that unhappy and embarrassing interlude. It had happened only the night before. He had taken Jennie out to dinner and had plucked up courage to pop the question between the dessert and coffee. If only he had made his move earlier, would her decision have been different? Had the lateness of his proposal made it appear too impulsive, too superficial, not founded on deep and serious consideration?

'Take your time, Jennie. I believe the Channel Islands are very different now from how they used to be when you knew them. There's been a war since then – the Occupation and all that.'

'John, dear John; I'm not so foolish as to believe that I ever knew Guernsey – not properly anyway. I was only a child in those days. No, I just have this feeling that somehow I might find a way of belonging there. You see, I've lost my roots, John. This way I might find somewhere that feels like home. I certainly don't belong on the mainland any longer, not in Guildford at any rate. Going back to Guernsey might just turn out to be the right thing to do. I've got to give it a try.'

Looking at John's so serious face, she had laughed and kissed him lightly on the cheek. 'Don't look so worried, John. I know what I'm doing.'

'I hope you do. I really hope you do,' he had said. 'Most of all, keep in touch.'

'Of course I will,' she had said; but apart from her phone calls just before she moved into Bangalore, there had been a depressing silence from Guernsey.

'Out of sight; out of mind,' grumbled John, who was inclined to measure out his life in similar platitudes. But now, at last, there was a letter and his relief was immense. At least his lack of enthusiasm had not done irreparable damage to their friendship. He unfolded the letter and began to read:

My dear John. How can I begin to describe all that has happened since I came to Guernsey? It has been like coming home after a long journey. I seem to recognise people, although I'm sure I've never seen them before in my life. It's their ways, their habits, their kindness – and, it must be said, sometimes their incredible narrowness. I recognise these characteristics from long, long ago. On balance, though, everyone's been very helpful.

As for the house – Bangalore – what can I say about it? Put it this way: when I came to Bangalore, I knew immediately and with complete certainty that this was where I could pass a happy life. I have never felt more at home in any other place – certainly never in Guildford (although I fear it may hurt you to hear this). You must make up your own mind about Bangalore, when you see it, as I'm sure you will soon. All I shall say now is that I was extraordinarily lucky to get it for the price. It has a curious, otherworldly feeling about it; yet it's comfortable and somehow familiar.

As you can imagine, I am up to my eyes with things to do in the house and in the garden. I have, incidentally, found a real treasure of a gardener – André – or rather he has found me. He appeared as though by magic on my second day here and comes in several times a week to keep things straight – and only charges me a pittance into the bargain. Funnily enough no one I speak to seems to be able to place him beyond the fact that he seems always to have been the gardener here. Not that it matters. What is important is that he's a conscientious old chap – and that's more than I can say about Mr Jenks. He gives me the creeps, I'm afraid. I suppose he's all right really, but there's just something I cannot like about him.

Must dash now, John. Do come to stay any time for as long as you want. Just give me a ring. I'm practically ready to receive boarders!

Yours, Jennie.

Who the hell's Mr Jenks? thought John. He could have wished her letter had been longer and given more detail. There was a lot in it that he found disturbing, but could not quite decide why. He sensed an unease in the letter that the mere words did not convey. Also there seemed to be something uncannily final about some of her phrases – *...complete certainty that this was where I could pass a happy life... I have never felt more at home in any other place.'*

What a strange girl, John thought, folding the letter up and replacing it in its envelope. What a strange, impressionable girl she is. He scribbled the date on the envelope, as was his habit, and tucked it behind the clock on the kitchen mantelpiece.

A couple of months later, John received Jennie's next letter. It was full of snippets of information about her house and garden. Once more he sifted through her words, looking for some sign that maybe her honeymoon with Guernsey was starting to wane – but it was in vain. Only in one paragraph, towards the end of the letter, did he detect a note of disappointment.

One problem on Guernsey is that there are two distinct communities here which tend not to mix socially – the old Guernsey families (of whatever social class) and the mainland immigrants. I'm not sure into which category I fit. I feel more affinity with the Guernseys, being at heart (and birth) a Le Prevost, but I'm sure they see me merely as another mainlander called Jennie James. Ah well, we shall see. I really don't want to become 'ghettoised' with the rest of the English, locked into their horrid way of aping the Thirties British colonial expat style of life; but the Guernseys are so withdrawn – mistrustful, even – and difficult to know.

At the end of the letter there was a postscript that John found especially intriguing.

PS Oh yes; I'd almost forgotten to tell you. Bangalore has sprung a bit of a surprise – a real mystery, you might say.

> *You remember my 'rooms with corners missing'; well, on closer examination it seems that some (well at least one) conceal small areas that are completely enclosed, like walled-up cupboards or tiny secret rooms. What were they called in ancient days? Priest holes, wasn't it? Well, I seem to have at least one such priest hole in Bangalore. Exciting, isn't it? More later. Watch this space.*

Strangely Jennie's attention had been drawn to these missing spaces by a dream which had striking similarities to the one she had experienced during her first night at Bangalore.

The same man – the one who had walked out of the trees, across the lawn and into the house – had once more come to Bangalore. He had followed almost the same route with the same assurance, across the lawn, but this time up on to the lounge verandah. Jennie was watching from inside the house, standing by the open french window which led out on to the verandah which her visitor was approaching. It was a still, warm, moonlit evening and the sea was purring distantly at the foot of the cliffs. She was looking out at her domain, enjoying the sheer tranquillity of it all, when suddenly the man had made his appearance. He waved cheerfully to her, as though to a well-known friend. She, for her part, had felt no resentment or fear at his unexpected arrival and had moved aside to let him pass through into the lounge. Without a word he had walked across the room towards one of the splayed-off corners beside the fireplace, turned back towards her, smiled and disappeared, as though he had walked through a non-existent door in the oblique wall.

Jennie awoke without the least feeling of unease and by morning she had completely forgotten her dream. In fact, it was some days later that she recalled her handsome night visitor. It was as she was considering the redecoration of the lounge and was standing, deep in thought, beside the oblique wall through which he had disappeared.

Suddenly every detail of the dream came back to her. She remembered how full of life and energy he seemed, sun-bronzed and with hair greying at the temples. He was not a young man, but one, she thought, at the peak of his maturity. She remembered how her heart began to race as she saw him approaching across the lawn – and as he brushed passed her, how she had almost, without thinking, greeted him with a kiss, as if he were a dear friend, rather than a stranger. And yet, there was no doubt that he was a stranger, although she could not deny the feeling that he was in some way familiar to her.

Standing thinking about the dream, beside the oblique wall, it occurred to her how accurately her subconscious mind had depicted every detail of the room. Only the furniture was different – sombre brown upholstery and dark stained wood, in place of her own light oak and floral chintzes. Then she realised that her dream contained the furniture she had seen in the room when she had first visited Bangalore – Mrs Grace's furniture, of course. In other respects, though, the room in which she now stood, was the room in her dream; its shape, its great Guernsey granite fireplace, the french windows leading out on to the verandah – everything the same. And so she could position precisely where her visitor had been standing, beside the oblique wall on the left-hand side of the fireplace – the position where she had seen him turn, smile at her and disappear through the wall.

The deliberate, purposeful way in which he had done this, suggested to Jennie that he had wanted to draw her attention to the oblique wall; and now, as she looked at it more closely, she realised that its angle was not reflected in the line of the wall in the adjoining room – the dining room. Here all the corners were right angles. Clearly she must have been aware of this before, but had never consciously registered it. In the lounge the oblique wall matched an oblique wall on the opposite side of the fireplace, but in that case the missing corner had a logical *raison d'être;* it had resulted from the angled entrance hall which adjoined it. Now she realised for the first time that between the lounge and the dining room there was a sizeable, triangular space, apparently within the thickness of the wall, that belonged to neither room.

They must have done it to preserve the symmetry of the lounge, she thought, but then why not make use of the space for a cupboard or something? There's never enough cupboards in houses these days. She began tapping the wall and sure enough there was an area, about the width of a door, that had a hollow sound to it. 'I thought so,' Jennie murmured. 'Once there was a door there after all. I bet there's a cupboard behind it. And if there isn't, there ought to be. A cupboard like that could be very useful, especially in the dining room. When I redecorate, I'll see what I can do about that.'

And there, for a time, the matter rested.

Chapter Three

At the far end of the garden, Jenks was swearing in patois. It was the language in which he felt most competent and the one he could use most fluently to express his feelings, especially when tackling ticklish operations, such as the one in hand – the uprooting of the thicket of brambles and gorse which had developed between the cliff-top conifers. This jungle straddled Jennie's eastern boundary and was, according to her, an eyesore and therefore had to be destroyed. Old André had other thoughts on the subject, but kept them to himself. Now Jenks was waging war on the thicket with ever-increasing venom. Jennie, who knew no patois, could only guess that he was swearing due to the intensity and tone of his voice. One word seemed to recur with tedious regularity in his outpourings. It sounded to Jennie like *boodiax*. Whilst she had not the slightest idea what it meant, she guessed it was extremely rude and was glad she didn't understand patois. If she had, she told herself, she would have felt obliged to be offended. As it was, she could hide behind her ignorance, protected from offence and the resultant repressive action that would have been demanded of her. A coward's way out, maybe, but preferable, she thought, to a scene with Mr Jenks.

Jenks had entered into Bangalore life at the instigation of André, who had very definite views about what was, and what was not, work fitting for a gardener of his undoubted talent.

'No, ma'am,' he had said with polite firmness, when Jennie had asked him to clear some of the scrub at the head of the cliff, 'that's not the kind of work for a gardener. I do know a man who is more suited to that sort of thing, though. I'll bring him along on Thursday.' And bring him along he did – on Thursday, and any other day when he believed the required labour was unsuitable for his own more specialist attention.

Whereas André exuded old-world charm and respect – somewhat in the manner of a long-serving gamekeeper towards his benevolent employer – Jenks appeared to hate the world and everyone in it. As far as Jennie could make out, he seemed to have few redeeming features. He was sly, never looked her full in the face and scarcely ever spoke and then only to André; never to her. In fact, all communication passed between her and Jenks through the good offices of André – an arrangement with which (all things considered) she was well satisfied.

The day was going to be hot. The light mist, through which the sun had made a tentative rising, was clearing from the cliff top and, even as Jennie looked out from the verandah outside her bedroom, she could see the horizon beginning to sharpen. André was performing some act of skill among the rose bushes in a bed close to the house, whilst Jenks appeared as a small, angry figure on the edge of the scene among the pine trees near the cliff top. From this frantic, distant figure flowed a succession of grunts and growls as he fought with the undergrowth which, for several years, had been allowed to take a stranglehold around the boles of the trees, creating a natural barrier between the garden and the public footpath which ran along the top of the cliff. This cliff-top footpath was said to pass right round the island, although Jennie had never found anyone who had attempted to complete the circuit.

At first André held his peace over the removal of the thicket. It was only after Jenks had been working on it for some hours that he muttered to Jennie in a conspiratorial tone: 'It do open up the garden, ma'am, to undesirables.'

'Oh, never!' Jennie laughed. 'What undesirables? Anyway it blocks the view and we can always replace it with a light fence, if we really find it becomes necessary. But so few people seem to use the footpath, I really don't think we need a barrier. I would prefer to leave it open.'

'There's always the holidaymakers,' explained André darkly.

Jennie had to admit she had not yet experienced a summer season on the island. Maybe her ideas would change then. Who could tell? She decided to shelve the problem until she had discovered what the summer would bring.

Suddenly there was a particularly urgent cry from the far end of the garden, and Jenks's distant form disappeared from view.

'My God, he's fallen over the cliff,' exclaimed Jennie. It certainly seemed that that was what had happened.

Together, she and André ran to the spot, where the figure had last been seen and found, lying in a deep hole in the middle of the thicket, an even more bad-tempered Jenks. André pulled him out of the mass of brambles and gorse, dusted him down brusquely and set him to work again.

'But is he hurt?' whispered Jennie. 'He seemed to be bleeding.'

'Them's mere scratches,' replied André dismissively. 'He's not hurt,' he added, as though the very idea of anyone like Jenks being capable of injury was inconceivable.

'But what is it – that great hole?'

André shrugged. 'There's plenty of them old defences all along the cliffs. 'Tis possibly one o' them. The Jerries made 'em – or rather their prisoners did – islanders, some of 'em, and other prisoners they brought over from Europe – Poles,

Slovaks, Ruskies. You name 'em; they worked on Guernsey. Crumbs, it were hard work making them bunkers – all hacked out of solid rock they were – and many of them prisoners were almost starving – no more than skin and bone. Some of them died as they worked, but the Jerries didn't care. Just kicked 'em out o' the way and left their bodies to be picked up by the corpse cart that did the rounds every night. Terrible inhuman it were. Treated worse than dogs, those prisoners were. Weren't prisoners really. Slaves, more like. I guess what we've got here is a bit of the German's defences.'

André had been clearly enjoying the more ghoulish parts of this narrative; Jennie was becoming increasingly upset. She didn't want this memorial to barbarity in her garden.

'But didn't you know it was there?' she asked. 'In Mrs Grace's time? Didn't she ever have the thicket cleared?'

'Not as far as I know, ma'am. And I should have known 'cause I worked for her ever since she came back to the island after the war.'

Jennie shivered. Despite the summer sunshine, she suddenly felt cold. It was inconceivable to her that such brutality could have taken place in her peaceful garden. The idea of prisoners dying at work on her land was grotesque. How could such horror be erased? Surely such acts must leave a taint on the place.

'Anyways, don't you be fretting about it,' added André brightly. 'We'll get the rest of the thicket shifted and then we can really see what we've got.'

André's supposition proved correct. When the brambles and gorse had been cleared by a bandaged and disgruntled Jenks, a small reinforced concrete gun-emplacement was revealed. Its entrance, on the landward side, had been walled up, but, facing the sea, there still remained a long, low slit, almost at ground level, through which guns had once pointed. Clearly Jenks had fallen into a sunken area created at the rear of the emplacement to give access to the bricked-up entrance door. A flight of concrete steps led down into it from natural ground level.

'What on earth shall we do about that?' asked Jennie, when she viewed the structure for the first time. She almost began to wish she had never suggested removing the thicket in the first place.

André shrugged his shoulders in a non-committal fashion, and said, 'That's dangerous, that is,' indicating the gun slot. 'Kids or animals could crawl in there and get trapped. I could get Jenks to brick it up, permanent like, if you want.'

'Yes, definitely,' Jennie agreed. 'It's certainly got to be made safe – particularly with the footpath being so close.' Then doubtfully: 'I suppose we could make a rockery out of it.'

And so it was agreed. On the landward side of the bunker, Jenks was set to work barrowing and tipping rubble to fill up the entrance hollow. Soil was then spread over the whole structure, forming a great mound, into which slabs of Guernsey granite were set at interesting angles to create a fledgling rockery. Soon Jennie's dark thoughts that accompanied the discovery of the bunker were forgotten and she was confidently looking forward to planting heathers and miniature conifers on her new rockery when the autumn came.

'You know,' she told André, 'that was the one thing Bangalore's garden lacked – a nice rockery.'

André, who didn't hold with such effeminate things as rockeries, replied with another non-committal shrug, and said: 'If you say so, ma'am.'

And no one gave the bunker another thought – not until very much later in this tale.

*

And so the summer passed in a pleasant haze of self-indulgent activity. Jennie spent time in choosing carpets and curtains for her new home, changing her mind a dozen times over this or that pattern, driving the manager of Lovett's Home Furnishers of St Peter Port wild with alternate spasms of elation and despair. At the same time as this, she was busily trying to visualise the colour schemes she would use in the major rooms, when the time came for the full-scale redecorations to begin. She had decided that the winter time was plenty early enough to embark on paper-hanging and painting. Then, when the days were shorter and the weather less congenial, she would not begrudge the time spent indoors. Anyway, the existing decorations were not too unsightly – harmless, if a little insipid. It was as if Mrs Grace, before she left, had had every room quickly freshened up with a coat of paint, and although the result was hardly to Jennie's taste, it was perfectly suitable to live with until the winter came.

One day Jennie drove her Morris Minor over to St Saviour's to take a look at the village in which she had been born and grew up. Her memories of the place were still vivid, although she had not been there since she was in her mid-teens. Surprisingly little seemed to have changed, despite the war, the Occupation and the consequent social upheaval.

She seemed to walk in a dream about those familiar lanes. She was a young girl again, seeing the places where she had played with her school friends, the leafy path behind the school where she had experienced her first clumsy male kiss, the cove at the foot of the Black Cliff where she used to swim in the turquoise water all summer long. Uncannily she heard her father's call, the one he used to summon his herd of Guernsey cows for milking, and she saw her mother, shopping bag slung on cycle handlebars, pedalling with great fortitude down to the one and only village shop.

But then the dream cleared and she was standing at the end of the track leading up to Slade Farm, her one-time home. Then the changes that had taken place over the years were all too obvious – two long glasshouses now occupied what used to be the Home Meadow between the farm-house and the road. Each year this field used to welcome the spring with a carpet of wild daffodils; now the white-washed glass of the tomato houses almost obscured the view of the creeper-covered farmhouse from where Jennie stood. But other things remained as she remembered them – the chicken runs beside the track, the sound of cows lowing from the byre behind the barn and that little window in the gable of the farmhouse – the window that used to light her bedroom.

If Jennie had been more courageous, she would have walked up the track and introduced herself to the present owners of Slade Farm; but that was not her style. Instead she had to be satisfied with the distant view of that little window and her memories of lying in bed on summer mornings, watching through that window as the swifts skirled in and out of the nest, high up in the apex of the barge-boards. Every year they returned to that nest, generations of little hyperactive birds, rearing a brood of chicks that, when fledged, fell out of the nest and instantly took to the wing like seasoned flyers. Jennie wondered if swifts still nested in that gable and if someone else delighted in their annual return, as she had done.

As for the rest of the village; change seemed to have been muted. The church, for instance, had remained completely untouched by the passage of time, except for minor dilapidations to the lych-gate and the inevitable extension of the graveyard, which now stretched away over an adjoining field towards the sea. Jennie found the grave of her grandfather and grandmother and laid a little bunch of jonquils on the untidy mound beside the headstone. As far as she knew, this was all that remained of her family in St Saviour's. There were plenty of Le Prevosts buried there, but Jennie could not tell whether they were relatives or not. Le Prevost was a common name on Guernsey, and particularly in that parish.

The door of the church was locked. Years ago a locked church door in St Saviour's would have been unthinkable; during the daylight hours at least. But times had changed, even if the outward signs were limited. Before the war in the western rural parishes of the island, crime was practically unknown. The tight-knit little communities were self-policing, handing out heavy collective disapproval to all transgressors of accepted norms of behaviour. Such society disapproval proved to be an extremely effective discipline. Cottage doors remained unlocked, windows ajar, day and night, and the church was always open. With a sigh of disappointment, Jennie turned away from the church.

She was just passing through the lych-gate when she met the rector, very out of breath and waving copies of the parish magazine in one hand.

'Did you want to go into the church?' he panted. 'Just had to pop down to see a parishioner, who's a bit under the weather at the moment, and I saw you looking round the churchyard from his window. Such a pity I have to keep it locked – the church, I mean – but you know how it is these days.'

'I'd very much like to look inside, if it's not too much trouble,' Jennie replied.

'No trouble at all. I've got things to do inside myself anyway. Come on.'

Jennie thanked him and found herself standing once more in the church where she had been christened and confirmed, where she had begun to sing in the choir just before her family left the island and where her mother and father had been regular attenders all their married life until they left Guernsey.

Why her father had decided to give up farming and move to the mainland, Jennie was never quite sure. Maybe it was a premonition of the coming war, maybe it was just disillusion with the hard life of a Guernsey farmer. Whatever the reason, the move had not brought happiness for her parents. Her father never settled to his factory job, although he earned good money, working long hours in the munitions race before the war. Then disaster struck. Both were killed in an air raid early in the conflict. Their little semi in Cockfosters was flattened by a bomb, jettisoned by a wounded German bomber trying to limp its way back to the fatherland. Jennie at that time had luckily been evacuated to Yorkshire.

Memories flooded back, as she stood in the church, smelling the familiar scent of dusty hymn books, wilted flowers and candle grease. She sought out the pew she and her parents used to occupy most Sundays and read the names scratched in the old woodwork by countless little boys during boring sermons. Some were new; but most she could remember having read before, all those years ago. Here she sat for a while, thinking of how her life had mapped itself out, and how it had brought her back to Guernsey again as though by some strange compulsion.

If Greg had still been alive, she would never have returned. He had no time for the Channel Islands. Coming there only once on holiday, he had felt restricted by their limited size and, according to him, the parochial attitudes of the people. But then that had been soon after the end of the war, when the island was still very drab, bled white by the experience of defeat and Occupation. His death, so early in life, had left Jennie free to make the decision; to return, or not to return. Whilst she honestly believed that she had always longed to come back to her roots – whatever that might mean, her motives in returning to Guernsey could have been more complicated than that. Maybe it had been necessary for her to make a complete break from anything that was associated with Greg and their life together. Maybe she felt a little guilty about Greg, and needed to forget. And so here she was; living on the island of her birth, in what was apparently her ideal house, and yet... She could not say that the experience so far had completely lived up to her expectations.

She was caught in the trap of her apparent Englishness – a mainland name, a mainland voice even, after living in the South of England for so many years. To be accepted by the real Guernsey people is not an easy accomplishment for an outsider; and to them, Jennie appeared an outsider. Equally she did not want to become a part of the English 'expat' set that lived a pale imitation of the life of the colonial English in Kenya or India before the war. This group had its headquarters in the Yacht Club bar and talked in overloud voices and in false and exaggerated upper-class accents. 'The braying Brits' Jennie had christened them.

'Are you on holiday?' The rector had returned from the direction of the sacristy and was standing at the end of the pew.

'No, no, I'm not on holiday. I live on the island – well I do now – in St Peter Port. I've come back home, as it were. I use to live in St Saviour's – Slade Farm – my parents were called Le Prevost.'

'That'd be long before my time. I've only been rector of this parish since the war,' replied the old man. 'There are, of course, a lot of Le Prevosts here still. Some could be relations, no doubt.' He fidgeted with some papers in his hand. 'Well I must be getting on. Do you want to stay a little. I can leave you with the key, if you'll lock up when you leave and bring the key back to the rectory.'

'Oh no, thank you,' said Jennie. 'I've quite finished. I just wanted to see the old place once more.'

Walking together through the churchyard, the rector said to her, 'I hope to see you again – maybe at one of our services. Our congregations are sadly a little depleted these days, but we pride ourselves on having a good sing. No "nonconformist whispering", as my old father used to call it, but good, raucous bellows of praise. It does one good to let one's hair down with a good bellow now and then. So sad about having to lock the church these days. There are so many strangers about, you know.' Waving his hand cheerfully, he turned down the pathway to the rectory, leaving Jennie to make her way back thoughtfully to her car.

Summer passed away and the numbers of holidaymakers, who filled the roads with their hired cars and the streets of St Peter Port with their bodies, began to decline. Autumn crept upon Jennie, taking her quite unawares with its flaming colours.

'I really will have to join some clubs, or something,' she said to herself as the evenings perceptively shortened. 'I must get to know a few more people.' She knew the Guernsey winters could be a little trying – never very cold, hardly ever a flake of snow, but day after day of sea mist and clammy greyness – a depressing climate if you spent too much time on your own. 'I must make an effort to get out and about more.' But events on the mainland were geared up to put her resolution on hold.

Chapter Four

It was during the autumn of this year that John Frensham suffered the first problem with his heart.

'Oh God, no; not that again,' Jennie had exclaimed, when she received the news in a telegram from John's sister. Immediately she envisaged a re-run of Greg's unexpected death. To lose a husband and a best friend within a little over two years would have been a cruel quirk of fate. Without a second thought she booked a flight to Heathrow, hired a car at the airport and was at John's bedside in Guildford in a matter of a few hours.

It transpired, however, that John's attack, though severe and disturbingly unexpected, responded quickly to treatment. He was left shocked and suddenly aware of human mortality, but at least alive. After a short time in hospital, he was pronounced fit enough to leave and an extended period of convalescence was recommended by his doctor. Jennie insisted that this should be taken on Guernsey and flew back to London again to accompany him on the journey to Bangalore.

'There really is no need to mother-hen me in this way,' John had grumbled. 'I am a fully adult male, you know, and I'm still a few years off senility, God willing.'

And so it was that, as the days shortened and the autumn colours were rapidly swept away by the Guernsey winds, John came for the first time to Bangalore.

Looking back on John's visit. Jennie was to reflect that nothing was ever quite the same at Bangalore afterwards. Possibly she had difficulty in identifying the precise nature of the changes, but changes there most certainly were. Individually most were small and insignificant, but *en masse* they became troublingly pervasive. At the time, Jennie attempted to rationalise her feelings, putting them down to the effects of the season. She had not yet spent an autumn at Bangalore and did not know the house in the time of sombre sea mists and capricious rainstorms. Yet, however much she struggled, she could not deny (to herself at least) an uneasy sense of isolation – despite John's presence – isolation and menace even. There was a disturbing change, too, in the Bangalore sound. Into it had crept a note of anxiety, typified by banging shutters and lashing tree branches, all serving to give the place a faintly threatening air, which had not been apparent in spring and summer.

There were, of course, the crisp, clear days when she and John walked along the cliff path and enjoyed the views over The Russel towards Guernsey's island entourage of Sark, Herm and Jetou. On days such as this, all thoughts of menace and isolation were completely forgotten – or almost so. Certainly John, not the most imaginative of persons, became aware of this intangible feeling. He raised the subject on more than one occasion.

Quite early in his visit he had said, 'You seem pretty lonely here. Doesn't it worry you – this isolation.'

'Oh what nonsense!' Jennie exclaimed. 'Isolation indeed! What isolation? With a main road passing right outside the house and neighbours on both sides, how could I be isolated? It's a detached house in its own grounds, damn it. Not a two-bit semi. It's bound to have privacy, but not isolation.'

'But that's just it,' explained John. 'When you're in your garden, you're hardly conscious of the neighbours. You could be miles from anywhere – no noise, no chat over the garden fence. It's not like Guildford at all. What's more, when you're inside the house, you could be on another planet.'

Jennie withstood the temptation to say how delighted she was that living in Bangalore was not like living in Guildford. She knew that such a comment would only cause unnecessary hurt to John. Instead she said, 'That's the way I like it.'

Yet she had to admit that John was right. This was one of the curious things about Bangalore – its privacy. Despite the neighbouring houses being perfectly visible from the garden, when one was in the house itself, there was nothing to be seen, but Bangalore's own grounds, the cliff top and the sea.

'Your neighbours don't seem to be overly chatty either,' John pursued.

'I've already told you about the two Guernsey societies and the difficulty of fitting into either. I suppose it takes time. Mrs Guilbert and Mrs Robilliard, the neighbours from either side, have been in for coffee and they seem very nice people and only too willing to help. It's just a matter of giving them time to get to know me and learn that I'm really quite a normal woman and haven't got two heads.'

'Well I suppose you know best; but I tried to pass the time of day with the old lass on that side yesterday,' said John, indicating a rather dour house of Guernsey granite appearing coyly between an overgrowth of shrubs, 'and she fled from me, as though she were in imminent danger of being set upon by a sex maniac.'

'Poor Mrs Robilliard,' Jennie said laughing. 'She probably doesn't know what to make of you – a strange man in our midst. She probably thinks I've taken a lover.'

'Chance would be a fine thing,' muttered John grimly.

Jennie ignored his comment. She wished she hadn't tried to make a joke out of such a sensitive subject. She continued, 'They're very conservative – the islanders – and they're not used to a man at Bangalore. I don't know how long ago it was that Mr Grace died, but I think Mrs Grace stayed on here by herself for a long time afterwards. It was strange, though; when the two neighbours came in for coffee, they didn't seem to have known him at all, equally they didn't have much to say about her. In fact, no one does, except Mr Johnson, the estate agent, who goes on about her all the time – about her and her good works. I suppose latterly she must have kept herself very much to herself – and I imagine the neighbours have got used to it being that way with residents of Bangalore. It'll take a little while for them to come to terms with the fact that they now have a sociable female neighbour living next door – not to mention an exceedingly chatty and (I hope) frequent male visitor.'

'Unfortunately, they won't have to get used to a permanent male neighbour – not as far as I can see anyway,' said John. 'The lady's heart is still implacable – or so it seems to me. In any case it's too late for this male. He's already plunged into a physical decline.'

Jennie leaned forward and slapped his hand across the dinner table. 'Stop it, John. I won't have you talking like that – even in fun.'

But for all the light-heartedness of this conversation, Jennie was conscious of skating around the mouth of a frightening abyss, ever in danger of toppling in. Why was she so afraid of more than a superficial relationship with John Frensham? This was the question she often asked herself, but could supply no credible answer. It was not concern over Greg's feelings that deterred her. She was sure of that. Greg would have had no objection, if she had been able to settle down with someone else. And who better than his life-long friend, John Frensham? No; the barrier was within herself, and an implacable obstacle *that* had turned out to be. Could it have something to do with her feeling of guilt about Greg? Yet, why this guilt? Had she not been a good wife to him? But still there lurked within her psyche the belief that she could have done more, felt more deeply for him, given herself more fully.

Later she mulled over John's words about isolation. Whilst she would admit none of this to John, she was disturbed that his words so closely matched her own unease. She asked herself whether she had been aware of these thoughts before John's arrival.

Somehow she thought not. It was as though his presence had introduced disturbances into her previously peaceful existence – and not only disturbance within herself, but disturbance from other sources, outside herself. Maybe even from her once so homely house.

Ridiculous, she told herself. How could a house have a feeling about anything? And yet... and yet after the restful ambience of the earlier days, the place had suddenly become faintly inhospitable. Was she going off her head? How could she even entertain such wild thoughts?

Maybe it was one of those special dreams that had something to do with it – another dream in Mrs Grace's deceptively lulling bed. But now for the first time here was a dream totally lacking in comfort and reassurance.

It was night-time and Jennie was in the lounge at Bangalore. The scene was the same as before, but now the autumn gales were driving flurries of rain against the glass screens of the verandah. The man – the same man – appeared once more from the direction of the cliff path, but this time he was not smiling. He seemed remote, showing no inclination to enter the house. He remained standing on the lawn, looking in. Soaked by the rain, his hair was plastered down to his scalp and rivers of rainwater poured down his rugged forehead.

It was not his appearance, more his expression that sent a chill through Jennie. How could she describe that look? Was it fear? Anger? No, neither. Could it be a mixture of the two? She could not tell. She searched his eyes for some sympathetic response towards her, but there was none. He was unresponding, standing on the lawn, as though he had been excluded from the house by some deep conflict. In her dream Jennie moved closer to the window, desiring to force a reaction from him. Their eyes met and in an instant she had no doubt about his emotion. His expression was one of betrayal – a deep and bitter betrayal that incised lines of disappointment and pain deep into his handsome face.

★

John, it turned out, was not to be a good convalescent patient. Now the crisis was safely behind him and he was beginning to feel more like his old self, he became restless and bored with his stay at Bangalore. He was unwilling to sit and read, or watch television, or play Scrabble or chess, although he had an ever-willing opponent in Jennie. One leisurely stroll a day, building up slowly in length and strenuousness – that was the discipline of recuperation to which he was supposed to submit. But very soon he was cheating, taking a liberty here and there and, when the weather was fine, prowling endlessly around the garden and cliff top like a caged animal. Jennie did her best to amuse him, rather as one would a fractious child. They went around the island in her Morris Minor, visited Castle Cornet, the Island Museum, the German Underground Hospital and all the other sights on the Guernsey tourist trail. Jennie was always willing to fall in with all her guest's suggestions, provided they did not flout the rules of convalescence. But John remained incorrigible.

Whilst Jennie liked him a great deal, this experience of an ailing John had given her a new understanding of the chasm around which she had been intuitively circling ever since Greg's death, especially since that embarrassing proposal of marriage before she left for Guernsey. Now there remained no indecision. She knew her intuition had been right.

His restlessness was at its most irritating on bad weather days. It was on one such – a day when sea mist and perpetual drizzle subdued normal daylight – that John's thoughts turned to Bangalore's missing spaces. He spent hours prowling around the house, taking measurements, tapping on walls as Jennie had done, examining plaster surfaces and looking for joints in the skirting boards. In the end he came to the same conclusion as Jennie. Bangalore had only one missing space and that was situated between the lounge and the dining room. It was behind one of the two oblique walls which complemented each other on either side of the massive Guernsey granite fireplace in the lounge. This was a particularly pleasing feature of Bangalore. It formed a comfortable sitting recess, off the main body of the lounge, which was too large to be cosy and contained the french windows giving out on to the verandah.

'What you need to do,' said John, who was always prepared to say what other people should do about their problems, 'is to rip the plaster off and have a look-see.' It seemed that he was almost ready himself to seek out a hammer and cold chisel and start the work there and then.

'I know very well what I shall do,' Jennie replied, 'in my own good time. I want more storage space in the dining room. I shall get a hole knocked through on that side and fit the space out as a cupboard.'

'But I'm sure there used to be a door on this side, into the lounge,' protested John. 'It would be an easier operation on this side.'

'But I don't want a cupboard on this side. It would spoil the sitting space in front of the fire. If I'm going to have to put up with all the noise and mess of making the alterations, I'd might as well have the cupboard where I want it, not just where it's easiest. In any case, the work will have to wait until I haven't got a convalescent staying with me.'

'But I could do it for you. I'm fed up of just hanging around like a spare part.'

'You! I've never heard such nonsense. You're at Bangalore to recuperate and have a good rest, not knock seven bells out of the place.'

John went on grumbling about it for some time, but as Jennie's mind was made up, he at last let the matter drop. Nevertheless, however unconcerned Jennie might have appeared, she too was becoming increasingly curious about what she would find in her priests' hole. Certainly there seemed to be an intriguing link between the walled-up space and the man in her dream. Since his obvious distress during his last appearance, she had become even more anxious to get to the bottom of this mystery.

As for John, frustrated in one direction, he turned his attention to the other Bangalore mystery – André. It had been his aim for some time to break through the barrier of unfriendly silence with which André protected himself from most mainlanders, whom he found uncongenial – and, particularly, from John Frensham.

'That man knows things,' he told Jennie 'You can see it in his eyes. He knows things that would make your hair curl, if ever you could break through his reserve.'

And so that became John's self-allotted task. Eventually, after a few weeks of persistence on John's part, André finally began to open up, his mistrust gradually worn down by John's persistent nagging. Unfortunately for John not much information came out, despite many hours of conversation. Jennie, at least, was grateful for John's new interest. It gave her more time to herself.

One day over lunch John said, 'I've been chatting to André this morning. He's a funny old cove and no mistake. I was asking him about the war and he clammed up completely. It was as though I'd committed some unpardonable sin. I suppose it could be a sore subject for many of them. But I never thought.'

'I wish you wouldn't talk about the war – not to the locals anyway. And never, never press them about what they did in the war. As you've discovered, they can be very sensitive. I don't want to lose a damned good gardener because of your clumsy muckraking.'

John shifted uneasily in his chair like a sulky schoolboy, but could not resist producing his most prized gem of information. 'Anyway, he did tell me that Bangalore was used by the Germans as a sort of command centre during the Occupation. I can't believe it's very likely. After all it's not very large, is it? Maybe he's got it all wrong, although he insists he's right. He wasn't coming up with any more details though – just vague comments about comings and goings and strange happenings. I wouldn't have thought Bangalore was much of a place for any sort of HQ. I can't think what the Germans could have used it for.'

'Well, I don't know and I don't care,' replied Jennie rather snappily. 'Now isn't it time for your nap?' Her abrupt change of subject demonstrated how little she wanted to think of jackboots striding about her Bangalore.

*

John left just before Christmas. Jennie had hoped he would stay for the festival. Despite his occasional tiresomeness, she had no desire to be left alone over Christmas and the New Year. During recent weeks, John's presence had taken up all her attention and now, with Christmas practically upon her, she realised she had made no plans. Now it was surely too late. Restaurants would be fully booked; other people's parties arranged and guest lists settled; no chance of arranging a party of her own. She made one last effort to persuade John to stay and celebrate Christmas with her, but his mind was made up. He had, he pointed out, to get back to the mainland and pick up the threads of his life.

'It's no good hanging around like a beaten puppy, hoping you'll change your mind,' he told Jennie.

'Change my mind? Oh not that again, John.' She suddenly became conscious once more of the void towards which his presence was drawing her. 'I thought we had come to an understanding about that. I like you – I like you a lot; but I'm just not ready for any big emotional thing, not yet. Maybe I never will be, after Greg.' Was she ever so slightly aware of being guilty of a tiny diplomatic distortion of the truth? 'Surely, though, we can stay friends – really good, close friends, like we've always been. But John, dear John, don't run away from me just because I can't love you. And please, please don't go home until you're really fit enough to cope.'

In reply John merely grunted and neither spoke for some time. At last he said, 'No; it's no good, Jennie. I'm not happy to be near you like this – and yet not be a part of you. Over the months, since Greg died, I've grown to love you – love you deeply. I'm afraid "good friends" is just not good enough for me, physical wreck though I may be.'

Jennie said nothing. His mood of self-pity irritated her. They were having a pre-dinner gin and tonic and stood by one of the lounge french windows. From here she looked out across the twilit garden to the dark silhouette of the trees bordering the cliff path. An owl flapped cumbersomely out of one of the trees across the darkening sky. She thought how much she loved the place, particularly as it had been before John's coming – and no doubt would be again after he had left.

John continued: 'Anyway; that's not the only reason I'm leaving.' He paused, searching for the right way to put into words what he wanted to say. 'I feel I don't fit in here. I'm not a part of your Guernsey life. I'm an interloper – a hanger-on. I think we have grown apart in the time you've been on Guernsey. I'd be kidding myself if I didn't notice your impatience with my stupid bachelor ways – an impatience I never noticed on the mainland.'

Jennie mentally squirmed at so accurate an analysis of the change she had noticed in herself, and had tried to conceal – unsuccessfully, it now seemed.

'Even the place, Bangalore, doesn't seem to welcome me in the way it obviously welcomes you. It sounds daft, put like that, but it's what I feel. The place disconcerts me. I don't know why. It's best I get back to Guildford where I feel at home. You know what they say; when you fall off a bike, it's better to get straight back on. Well, I fell off my bike a while ago. Now I need to get back on and see if I can still remember how to ride the ruddy thing.' He chuckled mirthlessly.

And so it was agreed. On a bleak early morning in the week before Christmas, Jennie waved John off on the Southampton ferry with mixed emotions. There was no doubt, however, about her dominant feeling. It was one of relief. Despite the social void of Christmastide, she was glad that now she could get back to normal Bangalore life.

Back from the harbour, she walked through the front door of her home and knew immediately that things were going to be better. The old cosiness had returned and the underlying stress of recent weeks had disappeared. Even the house seemed more welcoming.

'It's good to be home,' Jennie said, and then added, 'What a silly thing to say. I haven't been away – and yet with John here, Bangalore did seem a different place – as though the house had taken against him, and because of that, had grown less friendly towards me. Oh I don't know! You're talking crazy, woman. How can a house feel or do anything?'

Shrugging her shoulders, she set about making belated plans for Christmas and thinking about what she would do after the festivities were over. Top priority in the New Year was to start investigating the hidden space, get in estimates for fitting it out as a cupboard and then, when all the mess had been cleared away, start her delayed plans for redecorating Bangalore.

Chapter Five

After John left, Jennie experienced a short and unexpected twinge of loneliness – a condition that rarely troubled her. She found time dragging. Despite the irritation she had felt about John and his predictably prosaic attitude to life, she had to admit she missed him.

One benefit, though, of his departure was that now she had time to think, time to take stock of her new life and find out how she stood in the ebbs and flows of emotion that had been tossing her about ever since Greg's death – more particularly ever since she moved to Guernsey. There was no doubt about it; she had changed. Although John had explained their altered relationship as a process of growing apart, Jennie had no doubt that the change had been predominantly in her; not in dear, dependable and often infuriating John.

During this period of heart-searching, Jennie also admitted to herself for the first time the effect that her dreaming was having on her life; not a direct, tangible effect, maybe, but an insidious underlying influence. Stupid as it seemed, since she began sleeping in Mrs Grace's 'dear bed', her dreams appeared to be playing a disturbing counterpoint to her waking life. Before she came to Bangalore, dreams had meant nothing to her. In fact, she rarely seemed to dream, or at least hardly ever remembered dreaming when she awoke. But now, the longer she mused on her life and its accompanying sequence of dreams; the more she realised that in some strange way the dreams were complementing her waking life; not mirroring it, but curiously reflecting its changes in direction and its emotional highs and lows.

'Well, it's only natural, isn't it?' she explained to the gas stove, as she boiled a kettle to make a pot of tea. 'After all, it is *my* mind that's having the dreams, isn't it? They wouldn't exist without me. Therefore I'm in control, aren't I? Or a part of my mind is, anyway?'

Settled with her tea before a blazing log fire in her great granite fireplace, she idly wondered why her dream visitor had been absent so long – and why he had been so distressed when last he had paid her a visit. In her mind, she could find no reason for this. To her, he was as welcome as ever. Yet he seemed to feel excluded, locked out by someone or something outside herself. Maybe her mind was not in control after all; but if not, from where did these extraordinary images come?

Oh stop it, you silly woman. That way madness lies, she thought. Yet, if you really believe this rubbish, why aren't you more worried about it?

And that was true. Worry was not a problem at that stage; just curiosity.

It was about a week after John left – Jennie couldn't recall whether it was the night after Boxing Day, or maybe the night after that, but it was sometime during that dead period between Christmas and New Year – that her dream visitor returned to her – and this time there was no feeling of exclusion.

Her bedroom was awash with light from the full moon. It was swimming in a cloudless sky, its brilliance extinguishing, or dimming all but the brightest stars. Still in the eastern sky hung the Christmas planet, Venus, blazing strongly above the cliff-top conifers.

She was not aware of his coming or, for that matter, his eventual going, only of his presence, signalled by a deep tranquillity that suddenly wrapped itself around her. Now, clearly he was at peace with himself and his contentment spread, like a soothing balm, through Jennie's bedroom, enfolding her in its protective comfort. All, but one, of her senses were alive to his presence. Only her eyes were of no service to her. She could not see him, but she heard his movement about the bed, felt the undulation of the bedsprings, smelt his fresh-air, masculine scent, reacted to the touch of unseen hands and the roughness of his faintly stubbled cheeks. Most of all she tasted the warmth of a live man's lips. She felt no fear, no anger at his intrusion into her bedroom, no surprise even. It seemed inevitable that he should come one day to claim what was rightfully his – and, in this, her heart and body were in total accord.

A deep stirring of near-forgotten emotion swept through her, and she was again the young Jennie James, sharing her life, herself, for the first time with another human being in the blistering urgency of wholehearted love.

She recognised the state of heightened sensitivity she had known for a short time with Gregory, when they were sinking together in the tideway of first love. Then every movement, every shared touch sent shocks through her body, shocks that gradually diminished with familiarity, until they had almost disappeared altogether. Then she had been sure that these delights would never again be experienced by her. But now here she was once more on the terrifying roller-coaster ride, alight with the agony and elation of first love – blood coursing, heart hammering and skin taut with anticipation. And all the while, the Bangalore sound shrieked in agreement with her capitulation to an inevitable coupling – an act that surmounted all the flimsy obstacles that time and space could interpose.

She awoke, breathless and disturbed. A new abyss had opened at her feet, but this time there had been no skating around its mouth, merely a wholehearted plunge into commitment.

'But you're a middle-aged woman,' she told herself. 'You shouldn't be having dreams like this.' Try as she would, though, she could feel nothing but elation and pride. 'He loves me; he loves me,' she repeated to herself. Then logic interposed: 'It's only a dream,' it told her, 'a silly, stupid dream.'

But try as she would she could not put the memory of that dream out of her mind, or ignore the sensations it had aroused. They were more real, more vital than most experiences of her waking life. Throughout the day they continued to haunt her, and when she went to bed that night, it was with a scarcely concealed expectation – hope, even – that maybe her dream would be repeated – her lover would come to her again.

Whether he did return on that particular night or not, we shall never know. But return he did, intermittently, during the succeeding months, filling a gaping void in Jennie's life. Soon he was as much a part of her existence at Bangalore as the sound of the sea and the rush of the wind, as the call of the seagulls and Mrs Grace's big and exquisitely sensual bed.

Nothing at that time was well defined; all was awash with mystery and imagination; but what was quite certain was that from that night, when Jennie acquired her dream lover, her feelings of guilt over Greg were gone forever, swept aside in the turmoil of a new commitment.

During subsequent meetings of Jennie and her new lover, no words were used; yet despite this, a deep understanding developed and information was exchanged, from which Jennie derived the certainty that her dream-visitor was Charles Grace, returning to his 'two most cherished possessions', as Mrs Grace put it – the house called Bangalore and Mrs Grace's 'dear bed'. To these two he had added a third possession – Jennie James.

Chapter Six

In the offices of the estate agents, Johnson & Co. Jennie was intent upon a mission. She had sought an interview with Mr Johnson to obtain answers to certain, and for her, vital questions; and answers she was going to have, no matter what obstacles were put in her way. Whilst to some people unconnected with this story, her questions may have seemed a trifle insignificant – irrelevant, even – to Jennie they were important. And so she had the bit firmly between her teeth. She was about to commence an engagement which would develop into a long, gruelling and ultimately blood-thirsty struggle.

Her attack was launched obliquely, leaving Mr Johnson somewhat bewildered as to what 'the dear lady was on about.'

'When we met before, Mr Johnson, you said that Mrs Grace was a tireless worker in the island community; but I haven't found anyone who ever met her – apart, that is, from her immediate neighbours, and they don't seem to know a great deal about her. They're extremely vague, in fact.'

Jennie was relieved to have at last taken the initiative and to be voicing some of the inconsistencies that surrounded her acquisition of Bangalore; inconsistencies unrecognised or ignored by everyone else seemingly.

Mr Johnson appeared older and more haggard, than she had remembered him when they had met during her purchase of Bangalore. Although he had greeted her with apparent warmth, when his secretary showed her into his office, he did not seem genuinely pleased to see her and was somehow ill at ease. He shifted restlessly in his chair, referring over-frequently to his pocket watch, which was secured to a heavy gold chain that drooped across his grey waistcoat.

'She was, she was indeed; but you see, Mrs James, I was talking about before the war – when they, the Graces, first came to the island in the Thirties, you understand. She was younger then, more energetic, so full of fun. But then nothing was ever quite the same after the Occupation – for none of us, I fear.' There was an edge of wistfulness in the ageing estate agent's voice as he spoke the last sentence. It was as though he were talking of an Elysian time long gone – a time of moonlit evenings with the sound of the foxtrot and tango, maybe even the Charleston, drifting across well-mown croquet lawns. 'Never quite the same, but then how could it be?'

'Are you suggesting that after the war, when they came back to Guernsey, they lived like hermits at Bangalore?' suggested Jennie, perhaps a little too aggressively.

'Oh I would hardly describe it in that way, Mrs James. It is true Mrs Grace was latterly a trifle – er – reclusive, I suppose one might say. Certainly not the lively soul she had been before the war. But then she was older. So were we all – much older. The experience of war ages one much more than the effect of years.'

'Mrs Grace, yes; but what about Mr Grace? The neighbours don't seem to remember him even.'

'Ah, Mr Grace – well, that's a different matter entirely They probably wouldn't remember him, many of them, that is. You see, he never came back to the island.'

'Never came back! After the Occupation, you mean?' Jennie was completely unprepared for this bit of news.

Mr Johnson nodded. 'I don't know why not. Maybe it was his ill-health. Mrs Grace often spoke of his illness.'

'But Mrs Grace told me how much work they had to do to repair Bangalore after the war; how Charles Grace had struggled to put everything to rights.'

'I think you must have been mistaken,' Mr Johnson replied with an unexpected edge to his voice. 'Charles Grace never came back to Bangalore as far as I know. Mrs Grace, I expect, came back to prepare the property for his return, but by the time it was ready, I imagine it was too late and his ill-health would not allow him to make the journey. As I told you when we met before, he died a number of years ago.'

Jennie sat before Mr Johnson's desk, struggling to come to terms with what he had just told her. Only the sound of the seagulls, screaming as they wheeled around over the inner harbour just outside the window, broke the silence. She was trying to remember the words of Mrs Grace's note about the bed. Unfortunately the note had long since been destroyed. What had it said? '*...My husband loved the bed, almost as much as he loved Bangalore. You now have his two most cherished possessions.*' Yes, that was surely it.

His two most cherished possessions; yet if Mr Johnson was to be believed, Charles Grace enjoyed neither for the last decade or so of his life. What was more, he and Mrs Grace appeared to have lived virtually apart during these years.

Mr Johnson shifted impatiently in his chair, examining his watch once more. 'If there is nothing further I can help you with, Mrs James, I really am quite extraordinarily busy. I suppose it's a sign of growing old. Everything seems to take so much longer these days – and estate agency isn't the profession it once was. Everything now is rush and bustle, bustle and rush. There just isn't the time to give the service we once gave – and some of us would still like to give. But now the younger folk are beginning to take over and it's all rush and bustle, bustle and rush.'

But Jennie had not yet reached the nub of her enquiry. 'Well yes, there is one more thing,' she said and noted the uneasiness grow in Mr Johnson's face. 'I didn't intrude upon your valuable time just to gossip about the Graces.' Mr Johnson looked suitably surprised. 'I really wanted to ask you why your company's information about Bangalore neglected to include any mention of its basement.'

'Basement?' he exclaimed. 'A basement in Bangalore?'

'Yes; a basement – a very large basement, Mr Johnson – well concealed, I will agree, but a basement nevertheless.'

Mr Johnson seemed suddenly to have lost the power of speech. A deep silence grew once more between the two of them, leaving the cries of the seagulls and the hooting of the fishing boats in the harbour the dominant sounds in the office. Meanwhile Mr Johnson's expression passed from disbelief to blank amazement and then settled into a haunted kind of fear. The colour drained from his face, leaving the skin with an unhealthy pallor.

'But – but how can that be? We had sight of the original building plans when we compiled the data sheet. There was no basement shown on them and Mrs Grace never mentioned such a thing.'

'Well, there certainly is no doubt about it now,' declared Jennie with some force. 'Bangalore has a basement – a very large basement. How it got there, I have not the least idea; but I would have preferred that it wasn't there now. It runs under the whole of the wing on the right-hand side of the entrance, under the lounge, the dining room, part of the entrance hall and the kitchen. Quite a considerable size, as you can see, and obviously Mrs Grace, or someone else, has gone to a great deal of trouble to conceal its presence – and I want to know why – why it was put there in the first place and why its existence was kept secret?'

Like the gun-emplacement, the basement had been discovered as a result of Jenks's handiwork. Jennie had experienced some difficulty in persuading any local builder to take seriously her request to make an exploratory hole in the dining-room wall so that she could take a look into the hidden space behind. After a number of false starts and disappointments, André had volunteered Jenks for the job.

Why not? Jennie had thought. After all the opening has to be made by someone before I can decide really what I want to do with the space behind. Why shouldn't Jenks do it? The wall is just a partition. It isn't holding up the roof or anything. When Jenks has cleared the wall away, I can get a builder in to give me a firm price for fitting out the cupboard and making good the wall. That would be a far better idea.

And so in the early days of the new year, Jenks had appeared equipped with a variety of implements, mostly overlarge hammers and cold chisels, and set about with ill-concealed delight making as much mess and noise in the dining room as possible. After an hour or two of banging, accompanied by a counterpoint of patois expletives, he had knocked out an opening large enough to see into Jennie's hidden space. Jennie was summoned to inspect the works and was astounded by what she saw. Just inside the wall was a steel handrail, protecting an aperture in the floor, down through which disappeared a metal spiral staircase, clearly leading to a basement.

Because the original doorway giving access to the stair had been positioned, as she and John had expected, on the other side of the hidden space (leading out of the lounge), the handrail blocked all access to the top of the stair from the dining-room side, until virtually the whole of the dining-room wall had been removed. Jenks was issued with further instructions and recommenced his banging and swearing. Soon the full extent of the hidden space had been exposed to the dining room.

Then André was summoned from the garden to provide physical and moral support and the three of them, not without considerable apprehension, descended the stair. André went first with a torch, Jennie next with another torch and Jenks brought up the rear, muttering under his breath and obviously not at all happy with what was going on.

In the basement the air smelt dank and stale, but once they were standing at the foot of the stairs, Jennie was relieved to find by the light of the torches that the basement was completely empty; not, as she had feared, full of rubbish and indescribable filth. Livestock, too, seemed to be restricted to an assortment of spiders. Exploring her new underground kingdom, Jennie discovered that it consisted of three rooms, separated by heavy metal doors. The stairs came down directly into the largest room, which extended beneath the lounge and dining room. At one end – the end under the kitchen – a door led into a less spacious room; whilst at the opposite end – under part of the entrance hall there was the smallest of the three rooms. No logical reason presented itself for the space being divided up in this way, nor was there any obvious purpose to which any of the spaces had been put.

'Well, I'll be darned, begging your pardon, Mrs James,' exclaimed André. 'I'd no idea – no idea at all – there was anything like this down here.'

'And neither had I,' replied Jennie, who found the discovery disquieting and strangely distasteful. She looked round the bare, unplastered brick walls, the concrete floor, the unpainted concrete ceiling. 'What on earth ever possessed anyone to build a basement like this? It's just potty,' she said.

'If you ask me, ma'am,' volunteered André, 'I'd block it up again and forget all about it.'

'I think you're probably right,' Jennie agreed, as the three of them began making their way back up the stairs; but things are rarely as simple as they seem. Once she was aware the basement existed, her curiosity was awakened. She had to find out why. She remembered how, in the beginning, it had been her dream companion who had drawn her attention to the hidden space. What had he been trying to tell her? Had Charles Grace installed the basement for some reason? But why? It would have been a costly addition to the original building price. So it must have been intended to fulfil some important function. A dozen questions began nagging away in her head, and it was these that eventually drove her to consult Mr Johnson.

'It could have something to do with the Germans,' Mr Johnson suggested. 'The basement, I mean.'

'The Germans? How can that be?'

'Well, during the Occupation the Germans commandeered any properties that were left unoccupied – as well as many that were still in use, I can tell you. Of course there were a lot of properties, like Bangalore, that were left empty, after the English – the people from the mainland, that is – left or were evacuated. That was the policy, you see. Born and bred Guernseys, unless you were very special, or of military age, had to stay put. Priority evacuation went to the mainlanders, if they were lucky enough to find a place on the boats; but it was all done in a bit of a rush, as you can imagine. Mistakes were made. Some got taken who had no right to go; others were left behind. Some didn't want to go. They preferred to take their chance in hiding. That was a risky business, and no mistake. Few succeeded in remaining undetected. Some were deliberately given away to the Germans by their friends. Oh the heartbreak and panic of those times, it's still painful to remember. Harrowing – families split up; husbands, wives, children separated, sometimes never to see each other again – and all in such a panic and rush, rush and panic. Those who left could only take what they stood up in and one suitcase – their whole world in a suitcase – dreadful. Everything else was left behind – houses just as they were, breakfast laid on the tables, ornaments on the mantelpieces, beds unmade. You can imagine it, I'm sure. When the Germans arrived, there were some very rich pickings – very rich indeed, and no mistake. Priceless treasures just disappeared into thin air.' The old man paused, seemingly having forgotten what he was going on to say.

'And you're telling me that Bangalore was one of the houses left like that?' Jennie prompted.

'Of course it was. The Graces were English, you see. And he used to hold a government appointment, did he not? In the colonies, I believe. He was a prime target for the Germans.'

'And the Germans commandeered Bangalore?' Jennie pressed on. She had the feeling that Johnson, whilst being happy to talk in generalities, was avoiding talking about her house.

'Oh yes, most certainly. It was a quite important requisition, I believe.'

'Important? Important in what way?'

Mr Johnson looked even more ill at ease. 'I suppose for whatever purpose the Germans had in mind for it,' he said limply, pulling out his watch once more.

Jennie was starting to lose her patience with his evasions. 'And what was that, Mr Johnson? Look, I'm sorry to appear a bit of a bore about this, but if it's got anything to do with the basement, I need to know what happened at Bangalore during the war. I think it's a reasonable request. You clearly don't see it that way, which is presumably why you are not being open with me, but I mean to find out. Come now,

Mr Johnson, don't you think it's just a tiny bit unbelievable that anyone could buy a property with a huge basement, over half the size of the rest of the building, and be totally unaware of that fact? Was this why Mrs Grace was so anxious to sell to a non-islander – someone who could not know of Bangalore's history? Mrs Grace was evidently happy for me to remain in ignorance of the basement; but that is hardly fair, is it? I had a right to know of its existence. And now, after all this prevarication I believe I have a right to know *all* the facts, as far as they exist. So, come on, Mr Johnson, cards on the table.'

Mr Johnson, during the whole of Jennie's outburst, continued to shuffle uncomfortably in his chair, his complexion varying from bright red to deathly white and back again in quick succession. When Jennie stopped, he seemed disinclined to speak.

'You were on the island during the Occupation. You must have heard rumours – must know something. What is it that Mrs Grace was hiding?'

'Of course, of course, dear lady. You have a perfect right to know,' replied Johnson glancing hither and thither about his office as though searching for an escape from this questioning. 'But you see, I don't know.'

'Oh, come off it, Mr Johnson. You must know something. You're an islander. You stayed behind. You're a respected member of the Guernsey business world with your ear to the ground. Not much could have escaped you. It's not a big place. There must have been talk.'

'Talk, yes there was plenty of talk. All pretty ill-informed, if you ask me – ill-informed and dangerous. That's why it's better not to enquire too closely about what went on during the Occupation. People can get hurt – unnecessarily – unjustly hurt.'

'But if, as you suggest, the Germans installed the basement under the existing house, they must have had a very good reason for doing so. After all, it couldn't have been an easy job. It was a major engineering feat – tunnelling under the house, supporting the walls and the concrete ground floor. It would have been incredibly difficult. I can't believe it was undertaken without a good reason.'

Mr Johnson seemed to shrink behind his desk. He sat studying his blotter slowly and deliberately for a long time, then he said, 'In those days there was a lot of talk – and, as I said, most of it didn't count for much. There was even a tale that Charles Grace came back to the island during the Occupation – another that he never left. There were slurs unsubstantiated accusations...'

At that moment he was interrupted by the internal telephone on his desk bleeping. Picking up the receiver, he listened for some time and then said, 'Yes, Miss Le Prevost, I realise that. I'll be free in half a minute.' Turning again to Jennie with ill-concealed relief, he said, 'I'm going to have to cut this short, Mrs James. I'm already late for my next appointment.'

'I understand, Mr Johnson; but you were, I feel, just getting to the important part of your information. Can I make a further appointment with your secretary to continue this discussion?'

'I really cannot see it's going to get us anywhere, Mrs James,' he replied wearily, 'but if you wish it. We're dealing with a subject neither of us at this distance in time can appreciate – a period from which facts, real facts, are few and far between, far between and few. And I am so busy, so very, very busy these days.'

'But I feel I must insist, Mr Johnson. Surely you see that your company owes it to me. Having inadequately described the property in the first place, you and your company are under some sort of obligation. Maybe what is done is done. Maybe we can't do anything about it now; but, for my own peace of mind, I would like to know as much as I can about what seems to me a most unusual happening. And I would like to see the original building plans, too, if I may. You still have them in the Bangalore dossier, I assume?'

Hearing Jennie's last request, Mr Johnson visibly slumped in his chair. 'I suppose so; suppose so. Somewhere, no doubt; in the dossier.' His voice was little louder than a whisper. Then, seeming to recover his poise, he said with some petulance, 'If you wish, I suppose you can make another appointment, but what good it'll do, I don't know. Equally, it could do a great deal of harm.'

In the outer office Miss Le Prevost was smiling and helpful in marked contrast to her employer. 'Another appointment? Certainly, Mrs James.' She began searching through the pages of a huge desk diary.

'I used to be a Miss Le Prevost,' said Jennie, trying to establish a rapport with this woman, who was probably about half her age.

'Oh, really? I come from St Martin's and all my family has lived there for generations,' replied the girl. She had a friendly, open face and was obviously overjoyed to meet someone who was treating her as something more than a mobile attachment to the office furniture.

'Ah, no; mine came from St Saviour's,' said Jennie. Despite the island being only a few miles from east to west, the two parishes of St Martin's on the east and St Saviour's on the west would have seemed like different countries to their inhabitants in the years before the war. Girls rarely married outside their own parishes and to do so would often start ugly rumours about past lapses in virtue. 'They don't live on Guernsey any more,' Jennie continued. 'Only a few distant relatives, that I never knew, are still here, I believe. But there are lots of Le Prevosts on the island, aren't there?'

The girl laughed. 'Dead common, aren't we, Mrs James? Just like the Smiths on the mainland, I suppose. Would next Thursday at four o'clock suit you? Sorry I can't fit you in before, but Mr Johnson is very busy until then.'

'That would be fine,' said Jennie and left the office, still seething with irritation at Mr Johnson's evasive manner. Never for a moment did she dream that she was not destined to keep her four o'clock appointment the following Thursday.

Chapter Seven

The office smelt of dust and ancient tomes, whilst Mr Grindle, junior partner in the old-established firm of Grindle, Grindle and Grindle, solicitors of St Peter Port, looked too old and emaciated for his years. Jennie began to doubt her wisdom in coming here.

The truth was, she was angry, still fuming over Mr Johnson's unwillingness to open up about the history of Bangalore. Despite her initial satisfaction that she had at least succeeded in making a further appointment with him, she was still uncertain if she, unaided, could exert the necessary pressure to persuade him to divulge more information. She was convinced that at their previous meeting he had been deliberately wasting her time, talking about irrelevancies, avoiding the important issues.

'The silly man thinks that if he blathers on interminably, I'll simply give up and go away,' she told herself. 'Well, he's got another think coming.'

Jennie was in no mood to give up, despite his clumsy delaying tactics. She was offended that he had not made more effort to appear just a little contrite for the evident failure of his company to describe Bangalore adequately on its data sheet. He owed her this courtesy at least, even though neither he, nor his staff, were probably guilty of negligence as such. She felt she needed to give him a shock to jolt him out of his complacency. Maybe a bit of legal muscle would do the trick. To this end, Mr Grindle was hopefully to be her agent.

However, that gentleman (referred to by the aged clerk as 'young Mr Grindle') was not encouraging. In her phone call she had asked for an urgent appointment to discuss a problem that had arisen with her new property. He, because his firm had acted for Jennie during the purchase, had braced himself for a meeting with an irate and dissatisfied client. He anticipated complaints (probably ill-founded) about his partnership's searches into rights of way or other easements to do with Bangalore's site. Consequently the meeting had been arranged to take place within twenty-four hours of Jennie's request; Mr Grindle's view being that the nettle was always better grasped – and grasped as quickly and firmly as possible. He had seen it all before and was well trained to deal with this sort of professional irritation. When he discovered that there was no question of the competence of his organisation being involved, but merely a silly woman worrying about a basement that didn't seem to be doing any harm to anyone, he visibly relaxed and assumed the humouring attitude, which he reserved for his more stupid clients. In his experience, he mused, these usually turned out to be women.

'Mrs James, I realise that your discovery makes the sale a little – er – irregular, but I fail to see that you have suffered by this inadequacy in the agents' description.'

'It's not a question of suffering,' explained Jennie. 'It's just that it's not right. I don't necessarily blame the agents. They were probably acting in good faith and had no means of knowing about the basement. They were supplied with old plans which, on the face of it, appeared accurate. But I do feel the vendor, Mrs Grace, is at fault. I feel she deliberately misled me into believing there was no basement.'

'So it is against the vendor that you wish to make a claim?'

'I don't wish to make a claim against anyone,' cried Jennie, 'not as such. I want information. I want to know why this knowledge was withheld. Mr Grindle, it seems to me that there is a conspiracy of silence over the whole affair. I feel that Mr Johnson is a party to this and that he knows considerably more than he is telling me. Am I being unreasonable to expect an explanation?'

'A conspiracy of silence, eh? That's a trifle over-dramatic surely, Mrs James.'

'No it isn't. I'm sure it isn't. I feel I'm not being taken seriously and I have sought your help to put pressure on Mr Johnson to tell me what he knows about the basement, and if he genuinely doesn't know anything, to find out the truth from his client, Mrs Grace.'

'You wish some form of formal letter from us to Mr Johnson?' Mr Grindle looked distinctly unhappy. 'I really think you are taking this thing much too seriously, Mrs James. After all is said and done, you are not the loser. You have even gained more that you believed you were paying for – more potential accommodation, as it were.'

'Potential accommodation!' Jennie exploded. 'It's good for nothing – no light, no ventilation. It's useless.'

'But if I understand you correctly, Mrs James, it was properly sealed up and the decorations within the bungalow had been made good. It was only your – er – (not wishing to appear rude) demolition work which led to your discovery. Now had there been a structural collapse, or a health hazard resulting from a basement that regularly flooded, something of that nature, I'm sure we could have been of assistance to you, but as things stand, I really would advise you, Mrs James, to let sleeping dogs lie.'

Grindle knew that if she were to force him into writing the type of letter she wanted, the Rotary lunch next

Thursday – an event regularly patronised by both himself and Mr Johnson – would be a distinctly frosty affair. It would be so unpleasant – not the thing at all. And his practice did receive a great deal of work from Mr Johnson's firm. He must not allow this to be jeopardised, merely because of the irrational outbursts of a stupid woman. He had to talk his client out of this sort of precipitate action.

'In short, Mr Grindle, you won't help me?' Spades had become bloody shovels in Jennie's mind.

'It's not a question of not helping you, Mrs James. I am merely advising you that there is nothing to be gained from the course of action you propose. You have a very desirable property, for which, if I may say, you paid an extremely reasonable price. Whilst I admit the vendor should have been more honest, she did not lie; she merely neglected to mention the existence of a basement that had no doubt been walled up for many years. The point is, you haven't really suffered any physical loss or inconvenience. There are no grounds for a claim, and that being the case, if we were to write the sort of letter you desire, it would carry no weight whatsoever. I would counsel a more diplomatic approach to Mr Johnson. It is, Mrs James, when all is said and done, merely your curiosity you wish to satisfy.'

Mr Grindle had succeeded. Jennie left his office with her tail between her legs, feeling a little stupid, but still very aggrieved. Why was the world apparently ganging up against her?

★

During the winter months, André visited Bangalore's garden less frequently than at other times of the year. Nevertheless, when the weather was reasonable, he could still be relied upon to put in an appearance. Then he could be found undertaking the odd bit of pruning, or sweeping up fallen leaves, or similar seasonal chores.

Seeing his slow arrival across the lawn one day, Jennie called him in for a cup of coffee. At this time of year she missed the company his regular visits provided. Consequently she keenly anticipated his less frequent appearances as an opportunity to have a chat. They sat facing each other across the kitchen table, luxuriating in the aroma of freshly ground coffee beans. Jennie offered him a home-made cookie – a treat which André was never known to refuse – and they were set for a half-hour's chat. André's initial reticence with Jennie had now completely disappeared. He had been slow to make up his mind about his new employer, but now his liking showed in a softer, more talkative attitude.

After a thoughtful chew at the cookie, André asked the question that had been rattling around in his mind ever since the day the basement was discovered: 'Would you have made up your mind yet about the basement, ma'am – what to do with it, like?'

'No I haven't, André. Not yet. I really don't know what to do. I suppose I might brick it up again.'

'By far the best thing, if you ask me, ma'am. It's a rum thing though – no one knowing it was down there.'

'I'm sure the Graces knew,' said Jennie.

'You may well be right,' replied André. 'Though they might not have been responsible for it, if you take my meaning. It might well have been put there while they were away during the war – well, while Mrs Grace was away, anyhow.'

'What do you mean by that?' asked Jennie.

'They do say that Mr Grace came back to the island, while the Germans were here. Some say he never left the island at all – just made it seem that way – but I dunno. It's all a bit of a puzzle, ma'am. Why should he come back? It wasn't like young Fabrice La Page, the harbour master's son. Everyone knows that the English put him ashore to spy for them – and spy he did, very successfully so they say. But he was young – and an islander. You can see the sense in him coming back; but Mr Grace? He wasn't what you'd rate as good spy material, Mr Grace wasn't. Some others say he wasn't working for our side at all, but was an agent for the Jerries, and it was because of that that he turned up again.'

'Oh I don't think that can be right,' replied Jennie. 'Mrs Grace was such a nice person. I'm sure her husband wouldn't be a traitor.'

'I suppose it depends on one's point of view, ma'am – as to whether a person's a traitor, or not. But Mrs Grace now; there you are right. She was a lovely lady. I never could take to him though. Never made much of him, if you see what I mean. But they do say' – André was never one to leave a story half-finished – 'that immediately after he disappeared the second time (towards the end of the war, that was) all the chief resistance workers on the island were rounded up and either sent to concentration camps in Germany, or shot. And he'd know all their names, wouldn't he?'

'Why should he?' exclaimed Jennie. 'He wasn't an Islander, as you have just said yourself. He had no background here.'

'Ah, ma'am, but they do say that he'd worked for British intelligence before he came back – a kind of double agent.' André fixed Jennie with a triumphant stare. 'If he were, he'd know all their names all right, wouldn't he?'

'Ridiculous,' she cried, 'I won't hear such talk.'

'But you never can tell, ma'am,' said André, shaking his head sadly.

In the depths of her heart Jennie had to admit to herself that she couldn't tell. No one could. All she felt was a deep conviction that her dream companion was incapable of such treachery. But how could she really know? She told herself how often she'd been wrong in her assessment of the living. How could she be sure about the dead?

'But surely you never worked for the Graces before the war?'

'No, never; ma'am,' André said with great firmness. 'I was over t'other side.' And seeing the look of enquiry on Jennie's face, added, 'T'other side of the island. Only came this side after the war.' He smiled a knowing smile and nodded significantly, as though to indicate his move at that time had a deep and particular importance – an importance that even a fool would appreciate. Jennie, however, remained in the dark.

'How did you know Mr Grace then? I was told he didn't come back to the island after the war.'

'Oh he was back all right. Make no mistake about that. Because I saw him – several times. He'd walk about the garden and along the cliff path, but he wouldn't talk much. Not like your Mr Frensham, ma'am. Now there's a great talker. Always ready for a chat, he is; but Mr Grace now, I reckon he tried to avoid me. Don't know why, though.'

'Was he ill?' Jennie asked. 'Could that have been why you didn't see him much?'

'Not ill, as far as I knew. Not ill, as you might say, in the body. I wouldn't know about up there though.' And André pointed solemnly at his head.

⋆

Jennie wrote a letter to John in which she gave an account of the discovery of the basement.

> *So you were right about the blocked-up doorway in my missing space, but unfortunately behind that door lies more that I ever bargained for. Imagine it – a huge basement under the whole of one wing of the bungalow. Good God, it's half*

as big as the bungalow itself, sitting down there all the time and no one knew. Thank heavens it isn't full of rubbish and rats. That would really be a horror. As it is, we (André, Mr Jenks and myself) found it to be absolutely empty – but no hint of an explanation as to why it was put there in the first place.

Anyway, I've been trying – rather unsuccessfully, I might say – to raise Cain about it. I feel I've been misled. The basement was hidden away in the hope that it would never come to light; and now it has turned up, there seems to be a conspiracy not to give me any information about it – how, when and for what reason it was created. My solicitor thinks I'm mad to pursue it. He sees the blasted basement as an unexpected advantage; I see it as a deep and bitter sadness. It oozes misery – you know how places can project the mood of events that have happened there? Well, that is very true in this case. The blasted basement has taken all the pleasure out of Bangalore for me. Anyway, I'm still set on finding out more about Bangalore and its past. I feel I must. I have no choice. Stand by for the next instalment.

John read this letter with mounting disbelief. What on earth was the silly woman up to? What good could come from upsetting herself in this way? And he sat down straight away and wrote to her telling her just that. Meanwhile, on Guernsey, Jennie found herself again frustrated in her investigation.

Chapter Eight

News of Mr Johnson's death came to Jennie in an unexpected telephone call from Miss Le Prevost on Tuesday morning, two days before her scheduled meeting with Johnson.

The voice on the other end of the line sounded tense and charged with suppressed emotion. 'I'm sorry to tell you, Mrs James, that Mr Johnson won't be able to keep his appointment with you on Thursday. You see he died last night.' Her last sentence, short though it was, was cut even shorter by a stifled gulp. Miss Le Prevost was clearly close to tears.

Jennie suddenly became aware of a sensation of extreme coldness – not a passing, shivering coldness, the sort one feels when, as they say, 'someone walks over your grave' – but a deep, implacable coldness that numbs the senses – the sort of coldness a reptile must experience when the sun is withdrawn, forcing the beast into a state of almost immediate semi-hibernation. It was not the unexpectedness of the news that froze Jennie's thoughts; in fact, since her dream the previous night she had half expected to hear something of the sort. What really sent a chill into her soul was the memory of Mr Johnson's face, as she had seen it in her dream – a face distorted by some unimaginable terror.

She was so shaken that it took several moments for her to pull herself together. When she spoke again it was in a quavering falsetto, so unlike her usual cheerful delivery.

'Dead? I can't believe it. What a terrible shock. He seemed so... so well last week, when I met him. Had he been ill for long?'

'No; that's just what has shocked us all here in the office. He hadn't been ill at all. He was really extremely fit and active for a man of his age. It's Mrs Johnson I feel most sorry for. Last night she went up to bed, leaving him reading in front of the fire as usual; but when he didn't join her after about an hour or so, she went downstairs again and found him dead in his chair, just where she'd left him. It was a terrible blow for the poor lady.'

'I suppose it must have been a heart attack?' Jennie suggested.

'That's what they are saying, but until the results of the post-mortem, I don't suppose anyone really knows. The thing Mrs Johnson finds so difficult to come to terms with is the expression on his face, when she found him – as though he'd seen a ghost, she said. It was almost as though he'd been scared to death. But I suppose sudden pain can distort the features in that way.'

Jennie rested her hand on the table to steady herself. Miss Le Prevost's news had quite unnerved her. Its details seemed to match those of her dream precisely. Only one fact was missing, the fact which only Jennie knew – the sight that had, in reality, scared Mr Johnson to death.

*

This was the first dream Jennie had had in Mrs Grace's bed, which had not taken place in Bangalore. There were to be many more such dreams in the future. They would range far and wide, in time, as well as in space; but the dream of Mr Johnson's death was the first on this broader canvas.

Jennie was standing in a strange sitting room – a warm and cosy room, full of large Victorian furniture, rather too large maybe for the size of the room and therefore a trifle oppressive. In other respects it was a cheerful room with brightly polished surfaces that glistened in the lamp light. It was a well-kept room, too – a room that was loved by its owners, for time had been lavished on its upkeep. Its heavy patterned curtains were not drawn across the two Georgian-style windows, but were left draped in generous parabolas across the glass. In the grate glowed the remains of a fire. All seemed comfortable and at peace.

There were two wing chairs with chintz covers in front of the fireplace. In one of these sat Mr Johnson, his head bowed over a sheaf of papers that were covered with small and precise handwriting. From where Jennie stood, it was difficult to see if he were dozing, or totally absorbed in his papers. He was alone in the room and the rest of the house was silent.

Suddenly something seemed to disturb Mr Johnson. It was as if he had heard a noise, although Jennie had heard nothing. He started and looked up towards one of the windows, the one nearest where he was sitting. In that instant, his expression was transformed, as though by a terror so intense that its effect distorted and dehumanised his features. He gave out a strangled cry and fell back in his chair, eyes staring and papers scattering about the floor. There he remained, senseless and immobile.

Turning to the window, Jennie saw, on the other side of the glass, the face of a man she recognised from her dreams, the face of Charles Grace. His eyes were hard and bright, as they stared with hatred at the lifeless body of Mr Johnson.

⋆

'Anyway,' Miss Le Prevost continued, 'I was ringing to ask if you wanted me to re-make your appointment with one of the other partners, Mrs James? It can't be straight away, I'm afraid. As you can imagine we are in a bit of a flap here at the moment, but Mr La Porte is free next Tuesday afternoon, if that would be convenient.'

Jennie had to struggle to bring herself back to reality and answer the young woman's question. What was the point of meeting one of the other partners, she thought? They were all so young – unlikely to know what went on in the war, or be bothered with her eccentric enquiry. She made an instant decision. 'No, I don't suppose it would do any good now. Thank you very much for your concern.'

'I believe you were interested in Bangalore's past?' pursued Miss Le Prevost. 'I know Mr Johnson had been working on your problem since your last meeting, but he didn't produce any papers, as far as I know.' (Oh but he did, he did, thought Jennie, remembering the sheets of notes Mr Johnson was reading in her dream.) 'However, he did look out the original building plans for you. If you like, I'll pop them in the post to you. Also he talked to Clive Dumas on Alderney and I'm sure it was about your case. You know Clive Dumas, I suppose?'

'Clive Dumas, the author? Well yes, I've heard of him, but I don't really know him. He's something of an expert on the Channel Islands during the war, isn't he?'

'That's right. The other day Mr Johnson was talking to me about your appointment and suddenly he asked me to get Mr Dumas on the phone. It seemed as though he had suddenly thought that he might be able to help in some way. I didn't overhear any of their conversation, though. I wasn't in Mr Johnson's office at the time, so I'm not sure what they talked about; but I feel certain it was about Bangalore. Would you like to give Mr Dumas a ring? I could give you his number, if you wanted me to.'

Jennie thought that would be a good idea – and that was how, about a week later, she came to be sitting on an Islander flight, about to take off from Guernsey airport on its twenty-minute trip to the smaller Channel Island of

Alderney and her fateful meeting with Clive Dumas, the authority on the Channel Islands at war.

As she fastened her lap strap, one of the five passengers packed into the tiny cabin of the little De Haviland Rapide biplane which in those days made the twice-daily flights between the islands, she must have mused how it seemed that her relationship with Bangalore was becoming every day more bizarre – and more disturbing. What part, too, did her strange dreams play in the unfolding of the mystery? She had written down some of her thoughts on this subject in a letter to John, leaving out, of course, the more intimate sequences involving her dream companion. Part of the letter read:

It all seems very uncanny. I'm sure the man in my dreams is Charles Grace. Don't ask me why. I don't know the answer; but I'm as sure of this as I am of anything in this whole strange affair. It was he who led me to the blocked doorway to the basement and I feel sure he wants to tell me something about it – something to do with Bangalore's past. In a strange way I am certain that he had something to do with Mr Johnson's death, but I suppose you'll think me mad for saying that. My reason is a most strange dream about Mr Johnson on the very night he died and Charles Grace was one of the major players in that little drama.

It's all most strange, but I don't think I'm in any danger. Charles Grace poses no threat to me – quite the reverse, in fact. I believe that he is trying to protect me – keep me safe from some undefined threat that I used to sense quite strongly, but now sense no longer.

John had snorted as he read this part of Jennie's letter. 'What nonsense!' he exclaimed. 'The woman's clearly going off her bloody head.' And he wrote a reply, suggesting that the claustrophobic atmosphere of the Guernsey winter must be getting her down and would it not be a good idea to take a short break on the mainland, maybe staying with him in Guildford for a while? This letter had arrived just before Jennie left for the airport that morning.

Now as she sat on the Rapide, waiting for take-off, she tried to think objectively about what was happening to her. Her life on Guernsey was not the restful retirement from mainland pressure that she had expected it to be. Bangalore seemed to be consuming all her attention, and although she was disturbed by the discovery of the basement, her letter to John Frensham had maybe slightly overstated her concern. It was true she was aware of something unpleasant connected with the basement, but at that stage it had not become exactly frightening.

Other aspects of her life on Guernsey were disappointing. She was not fitting in to St Peter Port society as she had hoped she would. She was still very much an incomer and would probably remain so, on present showing, for the rest of her life. Was she worried about this? No, she couldn't say she was worried, although she would have preferred it otherwise. Probably it was this lack of real friends, which had left the vacuum that the disembodied presence of Charles Grace so adequately filled. But regarding him Jennie's objectivity was in question. She shied away from honestly analysing her emotions. Whilst she knew it was all illusion and would not bear a logical examination, she also knew what an important part it played in her present life. A door had opened in her emotional development, letting her slip back to her younger self, before the restrictions of Guildford married life had corralled her within middle age. Once more she thrilled with sensations and emotions she had not experienced for many years. But how could she expect anyone else to understand, when all was based on dream? Was she going crazy? The thought had crossed her mind on more than one occasion. But if this were madness, what delight it could be.

Her musing was interrupted by the plane beginning to taxi out on to the runway. The tiny biplane was buffeted by squalls as it took off and rose to its operating altitude just beneath a ceiling of scudding clouds. Below, the dark grey surface of the sea was peppered with white breakers.

In those days Alderney Airport terminal building consisted of a tiny structure, built of concrete blocks, little bigger than an average English village cricket pavilion, minus the verandah. Alongside was a miniature control tower and in front a mown grass runway, carved out of the rough terrain of the cliff top. This runway was the source of continual excitement for the intrepid air travellers to Alderney in those days. It was extremely short and ran at right angles to the cliff, its end identified by a couple of red and white markers. After these, the native undergrowth of gorse and bramble took over once more. A grazing herd of cows seemed to be the ecological means of keeping the grass of the airport under control, despite the ever-present danger of the animals straying out onto the runway at an inappropriate moment. Pilots of approaching aircraft had been known to make dummy runs at extremely low altitudes to encourage the cattle to keep a respectful distance.

A landing at Alderney Airport was always a thrilling (and, for the uninitiated, a truly terrifying) experience. From one direction, the plane seemed in danger of pitching into the sea before its brakes brought it to a shuddering standstill; whilst, from the other, the level of the plane's approach often seemed too low to clear the top of the cliff. Passengers new to a landing from this direction, or of a nervous disposition, often found the experience sourcing months of recurring nightmares.

Today it was a copybook example of this latter type of landing. The little plane flipped up over the cliff top, plopped down on the very end of the runway and came to a relieved halt about twenty yards off the scrub-covered land beyond the mown grass. The five passengers breathed a combined sigh of relief and began to chatter loudly amongst themselves, making light of the whole affair. Shared fear had obliterated their reserve and the five strangers, so stolidly silent up until that moment, became instant chums, who were quite prepared to pile into the solitary taxi outside the terminal building for a shared short ride into St Anne's, the only town on the island.

At the crossroads that marked the centre of the town, the four other passengers went their separate ways, whilst Jennie re-hired the taxi to take her to Fort Colombé.

'You're going to see Dumas, no doubt?' suggested the taxi driver, suddenly more chatty with only one passenger aboard. 'You know him then?'

'No; I've never met him before,' replied Jennie.

'Rum fellow, they do say,' commented the taxi driver. 'Comes here, buys the fort and then wants to buy the headland too – the one on which the fort's built. Well, that's not on, is it? I mean to say, the coast line belongs to us all. Part of our heritage, the coast line is. You can't have people buying up a bit here and a bit there, can you?'

'Can't you?' Jennie asked innocently.

'Oh well, you wouldn't understand, I suppose, being English.'

'I'll have you know, I was born on Guernsey of a family that lived on the island for generations,' Jennie responded with some heat.

'Sorry, ma'am; no offence intended; but you don't sound like an islander.'

Jennie laughed. 'I have lived on the mainland for an awful long time.'

'Ah; that'd be why I thought you was English,' explained the driver with some satisfaction. 'I'm very rarely wrong in these matters.'

After a pause, Jennie asked, 'How long has Mr Dumas been on Alderney?'

'Too long, if you ask me,' came the reply. 'Coming here, trying to lord it over us and take away our rightful heritage.'

And the complaints went on and on, until the car stopped at the end of a short track leading up to the ancient gateway of Fort Colombé. Clearly the driver had no intention of going any further. Having paid him off, Jennie walked along the track, which ran along the top of a short spur of land, connecting the headland, on which the fort was built, to the main shoreline. The sea pinched in on either side of this spur, making the headland into a virtual island, almost completely occupied by the ancient fort and situated between two wide and sandy bays.

In Napoleonic times the islands were under constant threat of attack by the French and Fort Colombé and a number of similar forts were constructed around the coastline to protect Alderney from their incursions. Now most of them were unoccupied and semi-derelict. Others, like Fort Colombé, had been bought by wealthy incomers and converted into attractive residences. Colombé was unusual in that it was one of the forts without an enormous barrack block, a virtually standard feature of most Alderney forts and one which made them quite unattractive and difficult to convert into anything, but somewhat austere hotels. And this was hardly a viable proposition. At that time, the island had few facilities and little to attract mass tourism. The large hotel chains were discouraged by its limited potential, short season, tiny size and tenuous air links with the mainland. Alderney's appeal was to the few, who were attracted by its isolation, tranquillity and bird life – not a formula likely to induce enthusiasm in large hoteliers. And so, many of the major forts continued to stand empty, gradually degenerating into ruins.

Jennie walked through the arched gateway into the inner court of the fort. This was surrounded by a collection of stone buildings that seemed to be sprouting naturally out of the rugged outcrops of rock which formed the summit of the headland. As she stood looking round, wondering which of the many doors to approach, one opened and there was Clive Dumas, a man in his forties with greying hair, a slight scholarly stoop and a boyish grin.

'Mrs James, no doubt?' he cried, clutching her hand in a firm grasp. 'So pleased to meet you. Come in and have some coffee.'

'Coffee sounds good. Thank you very much,' said Jennie, suddenly feeling that this interview was not going to be as difficult as she had anticipated.

On the telephone, Dumas had given the impression of reticence, but in person his whole demeanour was open and friendly. He showed Jennie into a huge living area with tall windows, overlooking one of the two bays. At one end of the room was a sunken area, containing a confusion of easy chairs and an enormous fireplace in which blazed a log fire. At the other, was a corner clearly used as an office, with filing cabinets, book cases, a plan chest and a gigantic desk with a modern electric typewriter. Through an archway on one side of the room, Jennie could see a massive rectangular, oak dining table, surrounded by chairs.

'Oh what a wonderful room,' Jennie exclaimed. 'And what a view!'

'Yes, it is rather grand, isn't it? The whole place is full of possibilities. I'm still working on the conversion, bit by bit, as I get permission from the Natural Beauties Committee – what a wonderful name that is, don't you think? Natural Beauties! It's the island equivalent of the mainland's Planning Committee, you know. Mind you, it can be a bit chilly in winter – the room, I mean; not the Natural Beauties.' He laughed. 'How do you take your coffee? White? Okay; hang on a minute. Make yourself comfortable by the fire.'

Returning almost immediately from the direction of the dining area with two cups of coffee, he said, 'First things first. You will stay for lunch, won't you? St Anne's doesn't offer many gastronomic delights at any time of the year. Out of season it's exceedingly bleak.'

'That's very kind. But I don't want to take up too much of your time.'

But already Dumas was walking back towards the dining area again. He shouted through the archway, 'Two for lunch, Jane, thank you.'

'Now then, about your little problem. By the way it was quite a shock about poor old Johnson, wasn't it? Nice chap, if a bit of an old woman. The first time I met him was years ago when I was starting to research my first book on the islands during the war. He was quite an important person on Guernsey during the Occupation, you know. He was a member of a sort of liaison committee of influential locals set up to try to oil the wheels between the population and the German administration. As a result, he came in for a few brick bats – accusations of collaboration and all the rest of it. Very unfair. It wasn't a question of collaboration, just a question of survival of the Guernsey civilian population. Many suffered a similar fate. A good example was an Englishman, the chief engineer of the States of Guernsey. He opted to stay on the island and face the Germans, because he was the only person who really understood the curious Guernsey water supply system. The Germans automatically interned any mainland English they came across, but they made an exception in his case. They had the wit to realise the stupidity of deporting the only man on the island who could keep the water flowing. He was much more use to them on the island and there he was allowed to remain throughout the entire Occupation, running the island's water – and came in for a great deal of unpleasantness as a result.

'Poor old Johnson. He suffered from evil tongues as well, and it made him very timid – very unwilling to talk – understandably so, I believe. At first, when I was researching my book, I had immense difficulty persuading people, like Johnson, to open up. I suppose in the beginning it was no help not being an islander myself; but eventually the penny dropped with them that, being an outsider, I had no axe to grind, not like some of the locals. At last they began to realise that they would get honest reporting, if they were open with me.'

'I had the feeling that Mr Johnson was just about to tell me something most important when our last interview was interrupted,' explained Jennie. 'Before that, I felt he had been very evasive.'

'That doesn't surprise me in the least. I would expect you to have had a bit of trouble with old Johnson – and how inconsiderate of him to die just at the wrong time.'

Dumas laughed happily and Jennie was relieved by the refreshing lightness that he was beginning to bring into her investigation. She had to admit, she had been becoming much too intense about the whole business. I've been treating it much too seriously, she thought and gradually relaxed in the comfortable armchair beside the welcoming Colombé fire.

'But what about your problem?' continued Dumas. 'I understand you have discovered a basement under your house that you and the estate agent's didn't know was there. Right? Johnson seemed to think it might have been constructed by the Germans and asked me to check it out on my maps of the German defences. Well, I drew a blank on that, from the address that he gave me anyway. So first let's check that I'm looking at the right house, shall we?'

At that, Dumas leaped up, collected a number of large-scale ordnance survey maps from his plan chest, brought them back to the coffee table in front of Jennie and squatted down to examine them. The maps were covered with annotations in different coloured inks.

'Quite a work of art, isn't it?' Dumas laughed. 'On these maps I've marked every German defence structure, command post, headquarters building, barracks and the like that appeared on maps captured from the German High Command. One thing you could say about the German army was that they were meticulous about their records. Now where's your house?'

Jennie pointed it out on the map and, sure enough, no annotations appeared anywhere in its vicinity. Even the gun-emplacement, that Jenks had accidentally discovered, was not marked. Jennie explained this to Dumas.

'Now that is strange,' he said, running his fingers through his hair. 'Without that omission, I should have been inclined to say that the basement was not likely to have a German origin; but with a missing gun-emplacement too... What was it like?'

Jennie described what she could remember of it; but now, concealed by her new rockery, the gun-emplacement was becoming increasingly vague in her mind.

Dumas looked thoughtful. 'Let's take a look at the options. In the first place the basement could have been installed by the Graces before the war. That's hardly likely, is it? Damn it; they'd only just had the place built to their specific requirements a few years before. Is it likely they'd suddenly decide they needed a basement? More accommodation, maybe? But not in the form of a basement – such a difficult and expensive thing to build as an afterthought. A second idea is that they could have had it put in after the war; but that is even less likely. I understand Mr Grace never came back to the island and why should an ageing lady on her own go to all that trouble and expense? Anyway, if she had, it would have been done relatively recently and would have been the talk of the neighbourhood. Everyone and his uncle would have known all about it. It certainly wouldn't have taken Johnson by surprise. Little escaped that gentleman as far as property on the island was concerned. According to me, there's only one other option – that your basement was installed by the Germans; but why was it not on any of their records?'

Dumas paused once more. The silence in the room was broken only by the sound of the breakers on the rocks below the windows and the crackling of the log fire. A faint cooking smell was beginning to drift into the room, making Jennie hope that lunchtime was not too far off.

'There is, of course, another possibility,' Jennie suggested, 'that the basement was constructed in the beginning, when Bangalore was built, but kept secret for some reason. I admit it doesn't seem very plausible and certainly there is no sign of it on the building plans Miss Le Prevost, Mr Johnson's secretary, sent me.'

'You haven't brought them with you, have you?' asked Dumas. 'You have? Great. Let's have a look.'

Jennie took the plans from her handbag and spread them on the table in front of Dumas.

'Where do you say the stair down into the basement is?' he asked.

Jennie pointed to the thickening in the wall between the dining room and the lounge.

'Yes; that is odd. Why on earth didn't they use it as a cupboard, instead of just wasting the space?' Dumas thought for some time and then continued, 'No; I don't think so. It doesn't seem likely that the Graces had it built that way originally; more likely the Germans did it. It's the only logical possibility. But why? There's no doubt they would have the means to do it. Think of all the slave labour that they imported to build their defences not to mention the underground hospital. They certainly would have the skill to do it. Think again of the underground hospital. Your basement, by comparison, would pose no engineering problem. Also, of course, they would have the means to keep what they were doing secret, if they wanted to – simply seal up the site and clear off snoopers in a way that the Graces could never have done in peacetime. No; the favourite option seems to be the Germans. But why? I should very much like to see your basement, Mrs James?'

'Do come and see it, if you want to,' Jennie invited. 'I should be happy to return your hospitality. But really the basement isn't much to look at. In fact, I am getting to feel quite foolish, making all this fuss about a silly basement. It's just that... well, it was a bit of a shock, buying a house without knowing it had a basement.'

But that was far from the complete story. And Jennie knew it. How, though, could she start to explain to a complete stranger the litany of strange happenings that had excited her curiosity, starting with Mrs Grace's actions on vacating the property and culminating in the discovery of the basement? Even more, how could she tell him of the persistent appearances in her dreams of the man she called Charles Grace? She hesitated, looked at Dumas's good-natured, cheerful face and suddenly hesitated no longer.

'Mr Dumas,' she began.

'Do call me Clive,' interrupted Dumas.

'Clive; can I be perfectly honest with you? I know it's going to sound ridiculous, but ever since I've been at Bangalore, the place seems to have taken me over – the place and a stranger who appears in all my dreams about the place – a stranger I have come to think of as Charles Grace, although I've no rational basis for that belief. It's not that

I'm unhappy, or scared, or anything very specific. It's just that the place seems to have a character which has totally absorbed me – and I just know the basement holds the key to some mystery that lies at the root of my obsession.'

Dumas nodded seriously. 'Places do have unaccountable atmospheres – all-pervading *ambiances* of happiness, or fear, pleasure or pain. Just think of the underground hospital again. When I stand in those galleries, I am consumed by a feeling of the misery and horror that went into their construction. It's practically tangible – as real as the rock and concrete. Places with very definite atmospheres aren't so bad. In their case you know immediately whether you like the place or hate it and you can act accordingly. But it's the more equivocal ones, the ones that give off less definite vibes, those are the ones that catch you out.'

Jennie was amazed how succinctly Dumas had described her feelings. 'Also I'm sure that my worries about Bangalore are connected with Charles Grace. There seemed to be some mystery about his death and his activities before he died. I know Mrs Grace was not telling the truth, when I spoke to her, and I suspect neither was Mr Johnson. I believe he never told me all he knew about Charles Grace and it was this he was about to do when our last interview was interrupted.'

And so the conversation drifted on towards lunchtime in a friendly, companionable sort of way – the sort of way in which Jennie had once talked with John, but now apparently could do so no longer. She realised that she had an unexpected rapport with this man, she had only just met; and as a result found herself talking to him with an openness and candour that she would normally have reserved for an established friend.

During lunch, Dumas brought the conversation back to Bangalore.

'Now I've got the measure of your problem, I'll do a bit more delving. I may come up with something. Who can tell? Leave it with me.'

'I don't want to put you to any trouble.'

'No trouble at all. It's a fascinating puzzle – and one I can't put down, now my curiosity has been well and truly aroused.'

Jennie felt the warmth of their friendship growing. 'I used to think of myself as very level-headed,' she said, 'not the sort of person prone to vivid imaginings and certainly not likely to dream up crises where none existed. But somehow at Bangalore everything is different. It breaks all the rules – sometimes it's happy; sometimes it's sad. I'm being tossed backwards and forwards from one emotion to another.'

'Does anyone else – your friends that visit you – feel anything about the place?'

'Well, I've only had one visitor – a friend of my late husband. He stayed for a few weeks before Christmas. He said he felt quite unhappy at Bangalore – threatened, even. I don't feel anything like that.'

Jennie realised what a relief it was to speak openly of her feelings about Bangalore. With John it had been different. With him she had been self-protective, anticipating his readiness to find fault with her new home and, as a result, anxious to counteract this with over-enthusiastic praise. But now, with this stranger, she was able to be totally honest – to tell everything – well almost everything – as she saw it.

Dumas thoughtfully chewed a piece of steak from the delicious stew that his housekeeper had just served. It was as though he were considering whether or not to say something more; but after a few moments' reflection he seemed to decide against it and merely said, 'Give me a couple of weeks and I'll get back to you. I'll ring you anyway, whether I have found out anything more or not.

That way I won't leave you dangling in mid-air, as it were.' He laughed. 'Now, after lunch, if you'd like, I'll give you a conducted tour of Fort Colombé, and then I'll drive you back to the airport.'

'I won't hear of it,' exclaimed Jennie. 'I've wasted far too much of your time already. I'll phone for a taxi, if I may.'

Dumas waved her objections aside. 'I think you'll be lucky if your flight takes off at all in this,' he said, indicating the rain-streaked windows. 'If I run you up to the airport, I can make sure you get off, and if you don't, you can come back here for the night. Much better than hanging about in that shed of an airport terminal on your own and then taking another taxi ride back to an inhospitable hotel in St Anne's.'

Jennie had been so absorbed in her conversation with Clive Dumas that she hadn't noticed how the weather had deteriorated. As the day had progressed, the squally showers had become more frequent, merging into longer spells of driving rain. The wind, too, had strengthened, lashing the water in the bay below Fort Colombé into a mass of white-topped breakers.

After the tour of the fort, they left for the airport. On the drive Jennie said, 'Fort Colombé is a really lovely place. You're making it into something quite special. But judging by the tirade from the taxi driver this morning, you have had your fair share of opposition from the locals.'

Dumas laughed. 'I most certainly have. I don't take it too seriously, though. The States of Alderney – the local authority, you know – were very happy to sell me the fort just to stop it becoming a total ruin; but they baulked at me buying that little piece of grassy headland just below my living room windows. I wanted it for two reasons: firstly, to give me a bit of privacy and stop holidaymakers peering in at my windows, their noses often literally pressed to the glass – and that's no exaggeration, I might say; secondly, because the chumps climb up there from the beach, when the tide's out, and then find themselves trapped by the rising tide and have to escape by climbing through my windows. Anyway, my request to buy caused an uproar. It all got very out of hand. Local protests, placards, posters, threatening letters, burnt effigies, the lot. So eventually I just let the whole thing drop and put up with the few holidaymakers that decide to make a nuisance of themselves every summer. You may have found the same sort of mentality on Guernsey. The islanders have very closed minds about many things. They resent incomers, but they want the wealth the incomers bring with them. And they can be extremely pig-headed. On Alderney, more than on Guernsey, I suspect, as an incomer you are very much an outsider. But I don't let it worry me.'

At the airport Jennie was relieved to see a Rapide parked by the terminal building. Yes, the airport officials said, the flight to Guernsey would take off according to schedule.

'Don't waste your time waiting,' Jennie told Dumas. 'I've interrupted your work too long already and you've been most kind and helpful. I can't tell you how much I've enjoyed today. Thanks for all your hospitality.'

'It was nothing. I wish all my interruptions were so enjoyable – and my interrupters so charming.' He smiled almost shyly at her as he said this and, when they shook hands, did he, maybe, hold on to her hand just a little too long? 'I'll be in touch, I promise. I hope you have a good flight, but I fear it may be a bit bumpy.' So saying, Dumas turned and ran back to his car through the driving rain. Jennie watched the car disappear down the lane from the terminal in a cloud of spray. Now that he was gone, she realised how alone she felt.

'You're the only passenger this afternoon, madam,' said the girl on the check-in desk. 'As you're here already, take-off will be in a few minutes.'

There followed a flight which, after it was over, Jennie did her best to forget. She had never been afraid in the air before and had plenty of experience of travelling in larger aircraft, but the return flight to Guernsey in the tiny de Haviland Rapide was quite different from anything she had ever experienced. The weather was still deteriorating and the flight took off a quarter of an hour early 'to beat the worst of the weather,' the pilot told her cheerfully, as they walked out together to the plane.

Once airborne, the Rapide was tossed about like a cork on a stormy sea. Almost immediately they were in dense cloud, which was suffused with an unearthly greenish glow. Alone in the passenger cabin, Jennie began to feel distinctly unwell. First she became abnormally hot, then a cold sweat broke out on her forehead; finally nausea began to well up threateningly.

'Oh, God; I'm going to be sick,' she thought. 'How embarrassing.'

She'd never before suffered the faintest trace of air-sickness. In a panic she looked round for a sick bag, but there was nothing in the pocket on the back of the seat in front of her, nor in the other seat across the narrow aisle. Oh, God: what was she to do? With great effort of will Jennie attempted to relax. She rested her head back on the seat headrest, closed her eyes, breathed deeply and prayed for the flight to end quickly.

She remained in that state until the plane touched down and bounced to a halt in front of the Guernsey terminal building. At last released from her airborne prison, she staggered into the terminal building and, leaving her car to be picked up when she felt better, found a taxi and was soon sitting comfortably in front of her own fireplace at Bangalore.

There she sat for a long time, drifting in that twilight zone between sleep and wakefulness. The storms had passed and now daylight was fading, but still Jennie did not stir. She sat, watching the leaping of the flames in her grate and considering all that had occurred that day. Now her nausea had passed, she was feeling warm and relaxed.

What an extraordinary thing, she thought. How ill I felt.

Now, as she closed her eyes, she sank back into the same semi-conscious state in which she had survived the plane journey. During that time, she had not slept; she could not have slept, feeling as ill as she did. All through those endless minutes she had been conscious of the pitching of the aircraft and the roar of its engines, as it fought to maintain its course in the turbulent air. Yet she could swear that, through it all, came a voice that must have belonged to Charles Grace. She knew this with complete certainty, although in her dreams he had never spoken to her. But now she heard Charles Grace's voice. It came, not threateningly, but quietly, earnestly, urgently.

Leave it alone, Jennie, it had said. *Leave it alone, I tell you. Don't pry into things you don't understand. You can do nothing now. Let it rest in peace.*

Now, relaxing in her favourite armchair in front of her own fire in Bangalore, she heard his voice again. It was as though he were there, in person, in the twilit room,

Leave it alone, Jennie; leave it alone.

'But how can I? You led me to the basement in the first place,' she heard herself reply. 'You showed me where the entrance used to be.'

No; not me.

'Yes; you, you. Who else could it be?'

No; not me. Merely an imprint of events from another time. Nothing more than that, came the reply.

Now, sitting in Bangalore, she heard again Charles Grace's parting words, which she had heard before, as the plane broke clear of the cloud and made its approach to the runway at Guernsey Airport. *In your search for truth, be careful you do not unleash the evil that lies within and beyond us all.*

Chapter Nine

André had taken to walking along the cliff path in the evenings, smoking his one pipe of the day and listening to the sea and the seagulls. It was a habit that started soon after the discovery of the German gun-emplacement. Not every night, but possibly two or three times a week, all through the summer, he took his stroll, unbeknown to Jennie, and every time he passed Bangalore he cast a glance at its lighted windows and speculated about 'the new mistress' and what she got up to, alone in the house which had always held a mysterious fascination for him. For he knew – how, precisely, is unsure – that strange things went on there – inexplicable things – particularly in the days of old Mrs Grace. And, for this reason, the place and its garden maintained a hold over him, which perpetually brought him back – as when the new mistress moved in. Then he had returned to seek a continuation of his employment, driven by two factors; his fascination for this strange place and his genuine love of the garden that, over the years, had become as much a part of his life as his own home.

All through that summer and autumn, his walks had continued, died off as the dark winter nights drew in and recommenced with the arrival of the lengthening spring-time days.

Normally, André had no time for these strangers that came from the mainland to throw their weight about, as though they owned the island. But Mrs James was different. He had not been at all surprised when she had explained to him that she had been born on the island, even though it was in St Saviour's, one of those barely civilised, western parishes, where they still believed in ghosts and goblins and from where he himself had escaped after the Occupation. They were both escapees, come to that, he and Mrs James. So he liked her – and that was more than he could say for that visitor of hers, him who asked all the questions about the war. That he could not abide – prying into what did not concern him. Guernsey at war was Guernsey business. The island and the islanders had suffered the Occupation – not anyone else. Only the islanders knew what it had been like and only they had the right to pass judgement: certainly not busybody mainlanders.

On the night that Jennie came back from Alderney, André took his walk as usual along the cliff path. After the rain and the spiteful, blustering wind of the day, the weather had suddenly calmed. As André explained to his tabby cat, the only partner in his lonely life since his missus died three years before: 'Weather's thrown up all the evil in its gut and there's an end of it. There ain't nothing left to cause trouble.' And so off he went on his walk, his pipe clenched between his teeth. As he passed Bangalore, he was surprised to find little sign of life there. All was in darkness, and yet the daylight was fading rapidly – so rapidly that André knew he would soon have to be off the unlit cliff path, if he were to see his way home in safety. The only sign that anyone was in the bungalow was the smoke rising from Bangalore's one chimney.

Suddenly he noticed a shape moving out of the shadow of the trees and across the lawn, his lawn, in which he took so much pride. It was the shape of a man, moving not stealthily, but with the assurance of someone at home in his surroundings and confident of his right to be there.

Mounting the steps on to the verandah, he tapped on one of the pairs of french windows and almost immediately it seemed to be opened from inside and the man passed through.

'Well I'll be damned,' André muttered. 'Who would have thought it?'

But as he made his way back home, it wasn't surprise that Mrs James was receiving surreptitious male visitors in the evening that exercised André's mind; it was rather the strange familiarity of her visitor. Where had he seen such a man before? At first he couldn't be sure – and then he realised that it had been at Bangalore many, many years ago. It was very like the man whom he had seen on many similar occasions when Mrs Grace had been living alone (as many said) in Bangalore. The man he had always believed to be Charles Grace.

⋆

A couple of days after Jennie's visit to Clive Dumas on Alderney, she drove out to St Saviour's once again. She had no definite reason for going there, just a nagging idea that, because her Guernsey dream seemed to be going badly wrong, she needed to stand back from it and try to put things in perspective. In order to achieve this objectivity, she knew she had to put some space between herself and Bangalore. Maybe, she thought, in the peace of St Saviour's, things might become more clear.

On the way she made a diversion, driving to a place she had loved as a child – a piece of common ground that ran along the edge of some of the highest cliffs on the island a wind-swept, infertile piece of land which grew very little but gorse and broom bushes and tufts of coarse grass. On this poor fare, a small flock of sheep lived and apparently flourished in the salt-laden air.

Here she parked her Morris Minor on the very edge of the cliff. Below, the sea was crashing against the rocks; overhead, the clouds were racing across the sky in a futile and everlasting pursuit of one another. The place was deserted. No one came to Corbière headland in winter time. By contrast, in the spring and summer the place was always packed with visitors' cars and screaming children playing hide-and-seek amongst the scrub. Today, though, the headland was given up to the sea birds, the ruminating sheep and Jennie's Morris Minor, gently rocking to and fro in the wind.

As Jennie sat thinking about her life and the misshapen thing it was becoming, her thoughts turned to Greg and how much she missed his companionship at times like this. And yet Greg would never have understood her feelings. He would have walked through the subtleties which she felt so keenly, as though they did not exist. Indeed, for him such things had no reality. It was not that Greg was insensitive, it was just... Sitting in her car, alone, on Corbière headland, Jennie suddenly burst into tears. She found herself longing for Greg and his uncomplicated, bull-at-a-gate approach to problems. In their life together this characteristic had so often had the unnerving effect of bringing events into perspective – making the horrendous seem trivial. She realised she had not shed many tears for Greg – only at the funeral really, just as his coffin had disappeared through the curtain on its way to the furnace. It was true she had been desperately sorry to have lost him, but at the time tears had seemed somehow unworthy and inappropriate for such a loss. Now, though, she wept with a powerful, uncontrollable dedication she had never experienced before.

After a little while she stopped crying and dried her eyes. 'What a silly thing to do,' she scolded herself. 'It was thinking about Greg that did it.' So saying, she realised guiltily that she hadn't consciously thought about him for months. 'Come on, pull yourself together, woman. This will never do. I didn't come here to feel sorry for myself. I really must make an effort to get my rag-bag brain sorted out about Bangalore.'

She thought back to the beginning – to the time when everything was new and perfect at Bangalore. She tried to recall how she had felt then; but it was impossible to recapture her old enthusiasm. Already it was history. Less than a year had passed, and yet events of that time seemed to belong to another existence. Had everything changed so much? Or was it her?

And when did the change start? Probably with John Frensham's visit. Poor, blundering John, (very like Greg in this respect) upsetting the tranquillity in a good-natured state of unawareness. After he had left, things almost returned to normal, but not quite. From then on, the basement had intruded, bringing in its train a series of worrying events; the horror of Mr Johnson's death, foretold in her dream; her own unhappy experiences on returning from her visit to Clive Dumas on Alderney; and that insidious, all-pervading feeling that all was not well. Precisely *what* was wrong seemed impossible to define. She was conscious of an utter bleakness, a lack of warmth and the loss of the old homeliness that once had been a characteristic of Bangalore. What was more, just when she needed him most, her dream companion, who always before had seemed to be spreading an invisible protection about her, had deserted her, adding loneliness to her other burdens. Silly, inconsequential things now troubled her. Was it her imagination or had the Bangalore sound become more menacing? And where had gone the delight she had taken in her own fireside? This had meant so much to her since her arrival on the island. But now, when she sat in the lounge in her favourite armchair, she was constantly aware that, on the other side of the wall behind her, lay the gaping void leading down into that basement.

The more Jennie tried to analyse her concerns, the more it seemed to her as though something or someone at Bangalore resented her having sought the help and support of outsiders – first John Frensham, then Mr Johnson and finally Clive Dumas. It was as though she was being told she should not delve into the past of the basement. She remembered Charles Grace's words: 'In your search for truth, be careful you do not unleash the evil that lies within and beyond us all.'

Jennie shivered. She suddenly realised she was feeling quite cold. Starting the car, she drove into St Saviour's village, parked the car outside the church and walked up the long pathway through the graveyard. Surprisingly the door of the church was open. She passed inside and was surrounded once more by that familiar churchy scent; this time redolent of Brasso.

On a sheet of newspaper laid out on the chancel steps, the rector was polishing the brass cross from the altar. He looked up as Jennie entered and smiled. 'Oh hello again; nice to see you back. And you didn't find the church door locked this time, did you?'

He looked a cheerful old fellow, Jennie thought; so down-to-earth and friendly.

'The ladies of the church usually do this sort of thing – and very well too, I might say – but sometimes I feel I should lend a helping hand. Some of my stalwarts have unfortunately been struck down by the flu, you see. Anyway, a few chores are good for all of us, don't you think?'

Jennie hesitated no longer. 'Do you mind if I talk to you, I know I'm not one of your flock and I'm not very religious, if you see what I mean, but I used to be a regular attender at this church when I was young and I do need to talk to someone so very badly. You needn't stop your work – and if you're too busy, I quite understand. I could come back at a more convenient time.'

'Nonsense,' he replied with a smile, 'never too busy to talk – and as for not being one of my flock, as you put it, I don't mind who I talk to. Talking's important. It's when you stop talking, the trouble starts. Too many people don't understand that my job's all about talking to individuals – giving them a chance to get things off their chest. That little bit of standing up there and spouting' – he waved his hand towards the pulpit – 'is the least important part of the talking I do. I often think my real job is practically nothing to do with religion and everything to do with life – and listening, listening to people who need helping to get things straight in their own heads. Then they often as not cure the problem themselves. So come on, how can I help?'

'Well, I think you may find this question very stupid, but do you believe that places can exude feelings of sadness, happiness, evil even? More than that – that places can influence how we feel and how we act?'

The old man sat back on his haunches and rubbed his forehead with the back of the hand that held the polishing cloth. 'I see what you mean; but I'm not sure I know the answer to that one. I believe a place can have a character, but I feel it's usually the character that we unintentionally give it ourselves – impose upon it, if you see what I mean.' He laughed. 'We humans are past masters at kidding ourselves, you know. If we feel a place looks dark and dismal, we convince ourselves that it has an evil air, whereas really all we mean is that it doesn't look pleasant. If we know a place has a reputation – if we hear that something horrible has happened there, we kid ourselves that the evil hangs on and makes the place itself evil, and that gives us the creeps. The human imagination is a wonderful thing, you know, my dear, but it can lead us a right old dance if we allow it to get out of hand. Have you got a place that you believe is influencing you?'

'I don't know what to think. You see when I came to Guernsey I bought a property that I thought was my dream house. It was the home I'd always wanted, but had never found. Then things started to go wrong.' Jennie gave a brief summary of the discovery of the basement and her subsequent unhappiness. She ended with a question: 'Should I give it up – my search for the truth about the basement? Am I stirring up evil that should be left undisturbed?'

'My dear lady, evil doesn't lie around, like a swarm of bees, waiting to be stirred up by the unwary. I don't think knowledge is usually a bad thing, provided one can accept the truth with an open heart. This brings us back to the imagination again. Imagined problems are usually worse than the real thing. And, as far as your problem is concerned, I don't suppose there is any going back now, is there? You'll never forget the basement exists – not now you know it's there. Better come to terms with it, one way or another.'

'I have these dreams about the wretched place, you see. At first, when I moved into Bangalore (that's the name of the bungalow) they were happy, comfortable dreams; now they have turned wicked and malicious. As though someone dislikes me – wants to upset me – do me harm.'

The old man rose from his knees with some difficulty and, taking Jennie by the hand, led her to the front pew. There they sat together, side by side, whilst he spoke words of comfort, so beguiling that Jennie quite fell under his spell.

'Dreams cannot harm you, my dear. They are just symptoms of your concern. I'm sure this is just a passing phase. You've had a shock – the discovery of this basement of yours – but the effects will pass. Most things do, you know, given time. Would I be right in thinking that maybe you have recently lost someone that was very dear to you?'

'My husband, Greg, but that was over two years ago now.'

'The effects of such losses often take time to come out; particularly when the grief doesn't show too much on the surface at the time. My advice to you, dear lady, is to try to get out and about more, maybe even go away on holiday, try to take yourself out of yourself, as they say; but what they precisely mean by that, I'm not really sure. Part of your trouble, as I think you know in your innermost heart, is that you are too much on your own – and during the winter, too, when it isn't pleasant to get out and about. It's always a bad time for those on their own. We have a few interesting things going on in St Saviour's. I'll give you a copy of our magazine. All the events are in there. Perhaps our organ recital the week after next might interest you? It should be quite good and there's coffee and buns afterwards and a chance to talk to a few people. You might even meet some of your long-lost relatives. I know it's a long way from St Peter Port, but at least you're sure of a friendly face here, now you've broken the ice with me.' He smiled at her, paused and then added in a low voice. 'If you would like us to pray together, just a short prayer or two; but there's no obligation.'

Jennie, who was no churchgoer, found herself agreeing. And, afterwards, as she walked away from the church, carrying a copy of the church magazine, her spirits were almost completely restored.

Chapter Ten

The voice on the telephone sounded excited, urgent – a voice with news to tell.

'Hello, Jennie. This is Clive Dumas. How are you? You must have had a lousy flight back from Alderney the other day.'

'You could say that,' Jenny replied. She felt an excitement so sudden and unexpected, hearing his voice again, that it quite took her by surprise. It was like a well-loved friend, dropping in for drinks, uninvited but thoroughly welcome. She found herself stammering, 'So good to hear from you, Clive. How are things with you?'

'Great, thanks. And I think I've found out a few facts that will interest you. Can I come over to Guernsey and take a look at your mystery basement?'

'Of course you can come – any time. I have to repay your hospitality, remember?'

'You don't have to do any such thing.' His voice sounded young and enthusiastic and contained a companionable chuckle which Jennie had not remembered, but recognised immediately on hearing it again.

'When would you like to come?' she asked.

A date was agreed for the following week and, as Jennie replaced the receiver, she was already making plans for a lunch, not too exotic, but hopefully a little bit different from the meals that one could expect to find in the repertoire of the average housekeeper – even a housekeeper as good as the one that Dumas evidently employed.

★

That night Jennie was visited by a different sort of dream. In all her previous nocturnal adventures, the action had had an obvious connection with herself and her life and emotions. Generally she had taken a part in their action, or at least was acknowledged by the other participant. The sole exception so far had been her dream of Mr Johnson's death; although in this case the repercussions of that dream had intimately concerned her, despite her passive role.

But now, for the first time, there came a dream in which the plot did not seem to have any immediate relevance to herself. She was merely an objective observer, standing about the set, invisible to the actors in the drama, watching them playing out a scene before her eyes, but unable to affect the course of events, or escape from the spectacle.

She was standing in her basement at the foot of the spiral stair. But the basement was not as she had seen it, empty and without apparent purpose. Now it was full of uniformed men, who sat at desks or moved about the room, talking amongst themselves or into telephones in a guttural tongue Jennie – herself no great linguist – took to be German. Maps of the island and the surrounding sea hung on the walls and in one corner a man with headphones sat intently at work in front of a bank of wireless equipment. The room was stuffy, smelling of bodies, sweat, dampness and an undefinable odour of fear.

Suddenly the door at the far end of the room – the door leading to the smaller room beneath the kitchen at the extremity of that wing of the house – was flung open and her dream companion appeared, accompanied by four armed guards. But whereas the guards moved with soldierly precision, their prisoner lurched between them unsurely, as though his limbs were being manipulated by some inexpert puppeteer. Jennie could not restrain the cry that sprang to her lips as she saw this pale and sickly version of Charles Grace. 'Oh my darling; what have they done to you?' she moaned. 'Oh my poor, poor Charles.'

The men at work at the desks paid no heed to the grotesque procession, as it made its way the length of the room and came to an imperfect halt in front of the door to the smallest basement room, close by where Jennie was standing at the foot of the stairs. Now, with Charles Grace no more than a couple of arms' lengths away from her, Jennie could see that he was unshaven and there was a large bruise stretching from his left eye to his jaw. She could hear his breathing in a series of sharp, shallow grunts. His eyes, half-closed, seemed about to be obscured at any moment by their puffy and discoloured lids. He was dressed in shirt and trousers, both dirty and torn. One sleeve of his shirt was practically severed at the shoulder.

The leader of the guards rapped on the door. Almost immediately there was an answering shout from inside the room. The procession entered and the door closed. Within minutes they reappeared and retraced their steps across the large room.

Jennie found herself following the party through the smaller room at the end of the basement. Here she was surprised to find the space divided by a heavy iron grill, which transformed the area into a minute prison and a larger guard room. On they went, out through a door in the further wall – a door that no longer existed in the present basement – into a long, dank passageway that must have extended beneath the garden.

A short flight of steps at its end took the party up into a gun-emplacement on the cliff top – the gun-emplacement that Jenks had so unexpectedly discovered. Out into a moonless night the procession proceeded. There, in the glare of a blinding arc of light, she watched as Charles Grace was made to stand at the very edge of the cliff.

The leader of the guards spoke to his prisoner, who appeared to answer with a weary shake of his head. Stepping back, the leader shouted an order. The three other guards raised their rifles, took aim and fired. The impact of the bullets lifted Charles Grace's body off its feet, throwing it backwards like a rag doll with arms and legs flung wide – backwards, over the edge of the cliff.

Afterwards, thanks to the alchemy of dream, Jennie was looking down the sheer drop of the cliff face and seeing at its foot the broken, twisted body of Charles Grace, lying on a projecting crag. Then a wave, larger than the rest, snarled up over the crag and sucked the corpse down into its anonymous grave.

Jennie awoke screaming.

Chapter Eleven

On the morning Clive Dumas visited Bangalore, the day dawned fresh and bright; but as the sun rose, there was no doubt about it – the first hint of spring could be detected in the warmth of its rays and the smell of growth that they conjured from the earth. It was either anticipation of his visit, or the presentiment of an awakening year that injected a lightness into Jennie's spirits, as she drove her battered Morris Minor to the airport to meet his flight. Once this lightness had been an everyday characteristic of her personality, but recently it had been considerably less evident.

Right on time the little biplane appeared at the end of the runway and bumped slowly over the airfield to its assigned parking place. The door opened and Dumas clambered out with the four other passengers with whom he had shared the flight. As Jennie caught sight of him, she experienced an unexpected explosion of happiness. A feeling of relief welled up inside her. It was as though she suddenly knew, with complete confidence, that everything was going to be all right.

For everything had not been all right at Bangalore – not for many days. Her dream of the shooting of Charles Grace had cast a sombre pall over her life, undoing any relief that she had felt after her visit to the rector of St Saviour's. For she had enjoyed a comparative tranquillity, after his words of comfort; but now that brief respite had only served to emphasise her recent switch of mood. Once more she was lonely and scared. The basement had become a yawning, omnipresent cavern, forever in her thoughts, forever lying threateningly beneath her feet – insistent, unclean and malignant. Now she saw clearly how, all the time she had lived in Bangalore, her contentment had been gradually seeping away – evaporating as surely as morning dew is dried by the summer sun. She could no longer disguise her unease, even from those, like John Frensham, to whom she had always presented an overly optimistic front, when writing about her new home. Suddenly, unable to play-act any longer, she simply ceased her correspondence. She did not know what to write about that was not negative and full of disillusion. And so she wrote nothing. Without explanation her letters stopped, leaving John bewildered and troubled.

As for the basement, she could not bring herself to descend again into its dank depths and had even found herself contemplating, not merely walling up the entrance to the stair, but filling in the entire basement with loads of rubble and concrete – mad and recklessly expensive, of course, but just what she longed to do – to destroy that evil place once and for all.

Now, though, as she saw Dumas's cheery face, his friendly wave as he noticed her waiting for him, relief surged up within her and she had to restrain herself from running to meet him and throwing her arms around his neck, like a love-sick girl. He, too, seemed to be gripped by some huge excitement.

'Have I got things to tell you!' he cried, as he shook her hand. 'You'd never believe it, how people suddenly open up for no apparent reason after years of stubborn silence.' But that was all he would say until they were sipping coffee in front of the lounge fire at Bangalore. 'It's too good a story to spoil by trying to tell it whilst we're ricocheting down Guernsey lanes,' he had told her and then, as an apparent after-thought, said, 'No disrespect to your driving intended.' But now, looking out over the lawns, dappled with weak sunshine, the time had come for his big revelations.

'First of all,' he explained, 'I thought I'd try searching again through the usual sources of information about the German Occupation. You know what I mean – original documents, military maps, eyewitness reports, survivors of the Occupation, all that sort of thing. I'd raked through most of this stuff pretty thoroughly before, when I was researching my books on the islands at war; but I thought there might have been something there that I'd overlooked. Anyway, that was a thorough waste of time. I found nothing that was relevant to your problem. Then it occurred to me that I was looking in the wrong place entirely.'

He paused, smiling triumphantly at Jennie. She offered him another coffee, which he eagerly accepted. As she fetched it from the kitchen, he roamed about the lounge, peering through its french windows.

'I do like this house,' he told her. 'Its views are magnificent.'

Jennie laughed. 'Not a patch on Fort Colombé. You're just being kind to my poor little home.'

'No I'm not. I can quite see why you thought this was your dream house.'

Jennie smiled sadly, noting his use of the past tense. Dumas reached out and squeezed her arm. 'Never mind,' he told her. 'It'll be like that again soon. Believe me.'

There was a pause and then Dumas continued his report.

'If we're right, about the Germans using this place as a sort of headquarters, there could be one very good reason why it was not documented in the official dossiers. This was the crucial fact I had overlooked before. You see Hitler's Reich was founded on secrecy and fear; the fear being largely generated by the uncertainty of whom you could trust, and whom you couldn't. Essential to this tyranny of terror were dozens of clandestine groups, whose *raison d'être* was essentially to spy on other members of German society – and later the societies of occupied territories. Hitler's security depended on them. They were to a degree remote from the main war effort; they formed a great subterranean network by which the leaders of the Third Reich could control and subdue opposition particularly amongst their own people. We tend to forget this aspect of the Germany of those days. We get obsessed by the international war and forget the war within – the war Hitler and his gang were continually fighting to maintain their position at home. You see, having achieved power, they had to expend enormous effort and resources in order to make sure they were not supplanted from inside their own state. Their strategy was to subdue opposition, even before it surfaced – and to do this they needed intelligence – the best intelligence they could get – and this came from the so-called Clandestines.'

Dumas was warming to his subject. He paced backwards and forwards across the lounge, as he spoke.

'These Clandestines were not under the control of the German High Command and their activities (even their very existence) were often unknown to it, until something went badly wrong, treachery was suspected and the Gestapo was tipped off and vengeance wreaked on the alleged traitors. Because of the type of work they did and the secrecy surrounding it, their activities would have remained largely undocumented – unlike those of the Gestapo, which tended to be considerably more overt. For instance, the populace at large had no doubt about the existence of the Gestapo; by contrast, most never knew anything about the Clandestines. Here's another idea for you to consider; have you ever thought who was keeping an eye on the Gestapo?' Dumas laughed. 'Oh yes; don't look so quizzical. I assure you it was very necessary. Hitler could trust no one, not even his closest collaborators, like Himmler.'

Once more Clive Dumas paused in his story, as though searching his memory for something. Then he said, 'Who was it who said something like "Large fleas have small fleas on their back to bite them, small fleas have smaller fleas and so ad infinitum"? Well, that was Hitler's Reich to a T. Someone had to spy on everyone, even the Gestapo; otherwise Hitler was never quite sure who were loyal. Possibly many clandestine organisations were so secret that even the Gestapo was hardly aware of their existence.'

Jennie listened, fascinated. 'What an extraordinary situation!' she exclaimed.

'Certainly was,' Dumas agreed. 'There is no well-substantiated evidence of any clandestine groups actually at work on Guernsey. But the more I thought about it, the more a voice inside me kept yelling; "Why not?" Wasn't Guernsey the ideal place for such a group to be established? If and when Hitler launched his invasion of Britain, the tentacles of the Clandestines would have to be operating on mainland Britain from day one. It would have been uncharacteristic of Hitler's gang not to have laid the foundations for such a group – established an HQ even; and where more logical than on Guernsey – an offshore island, out of the glare of publicity, a place where agents could come and go without attracting too much attention and from where England could be more easily infiltrated. There was another reason for using Guernsey for this purpose. After the Occupation, Guernsey was in a front-line position – a position where the English espionage machine would be likely to be hard at work trying to subvert German nationals, based on the island, in order to gather information and construct routes into German intelligence – hence the need for an anti-espionage group here. "Why Guernsey?" you may say. "Why not Jersey?" I believe that the very fact of Guernsey being smaller and less sophisticated, would have commended it – for secrecy's sake, if for no other reason. Guernsey was ideal; small, but not too small like Alderney. It had a good airfield and a sheltered harbour. Guernsey was so ideal, in fact, that I wouldn't put it past the Reichstag mob to have had it marked down right from the beginning of the war, or even before. Maybe there was a clandestine organisation in place here years before 1939.'

Dumas threw himself back in his armchair with a satisfied smile on his face. His expression was reminiscent of a stage magician, who'd just pulled off an extremely clever trick.

'Yes, I see,' said Jennie. She sounded lacking in conviction. 'But what does all this mean? Are you telling me Bangalore could have been the HQ of such a Clandestine?'

'No idea,' replied Dumas, happily, 'but it seems an attractive possibility, don't you think? Anyway it did start me off on an entirely different line of research.' He paused, took a quick look at his watch and said, 'But before I say anything more, I'd like to see your basement, if I may. Then, we've got to go and pay someone a visit. Going to be a busy day, I fear. By the way, I'm not returning to Alderney tonight – too much to do. Can we call up an hotel and book me a room?'

'I won't hear of you staying in an hotel,' Jenny protested. 'I've got a spare bedroom here. You'll stay with me, won't you?'

And so it was agreed. The special lunch that Jennie had planned for Clive Dumas was quickly rescheduled as dinner and, whilst Dumas examined the basement, Jennie busied herself preparing a bedroom for him. She was quite grateful for this activity. It gave her an excuse not to have to accompany him down into that depressing place.

*

When Dumas eventually emerged from the basement, his triumphant expression was even more marked.

'Someone's done an amazing job down there,' he exclaimed, 'at clearing up, I mean. Clean as a whistle – or nearly so.'

'What do you mean?' asked Jennie.

'Practically every sign of whatever the place was once used for has been removed, but not quite all is lost. There are a few tell-tale signs.' He pulled a notebook from his pocket and flipped it open. 'Firstly, the walls in the big room are covered with marks where things have been fixed at some time – shelves, benches, tables, that sort of thing. All the bigger fixings have been taken out and the holes made good, but the patches are still there for anyone to see, if you know what you're looking for. It seems as though once there was something – a bench or something at table height – running right round the room. Above this, I guess, there were other smaller fixtures – shelves, pictures or maps. There's nothing else in the big room – not that I can see by the light of my torch anyway. It might pay to get some better illumination down there, but I don't think there's much more to see.

'The little room under the entrance hall is pretty uninteresting. Nothing in there but a few fairly random fixings in the walls. It's at the other end, though, where things start to get really fascinating.'

Jennie had a strong suspicion that she knew what was coming.

'That room, under the kitchen, was once divided into two. I can quite clearly make out a row of patches, one in the floor, one in the ceiling, on the line of some sort of partition, which has been removed. This ran across the room from the wall under the gable at the end of that wing.

I can't tell anything about this partition, or why it should have been dismantled, but obviously that end room had once been divided in two. The most intriguing thing, though, is that at one time there was a doorway in the end wall. You can quite clearly see where newer brickwork has been pieced into the old brickwork, at some time when the doorway was blocked up.'

Jennie, who had been standing by one of the french windows leading out on to the verandah, turned suddenly and sank into a chair.

'I say, are you all right?' Dumas asked.

Jennie nodded. 'Yes, quite all right. I just came over a bit dizzy. You see what you've just told me gave me a bit of a shock.' And then she told him about her dream of the shooting of Charles Grace. She recounted the dream slowly, carefully, leaving no detail out. When she had finished, they sat looking at one another for a time in silence.

'Well, I'm damned; that is uncanny, isn't it?' said Dumas at last. 'If your dream is as accurate in things we don't know about, as it appears to be in things that we think we know, there is or was a passage under your garden, leading from that door out of the basement to the gun-emplacement on the cliff. That makes a lot of sense, when you think about it. That spiral stair could hardly have been the main entrance into the nerve-centre of the organisation, if that's what your basement really was. I bet the gun-emplacement was the main entrance – well concealed by undergrowth and trees – leading to an underground passage and by that means into the basement. The room at the end of the wing would be some sort of guard room. It all makes sense.'

He paused, apparently deep in thought. 'You know, I'm not an expert in building construction, but the more I look at that basement, the more it seems to me that it wasn't added on as an after-thought. It's much too tidy. I can't help thinking Bangalore has always had a basement.' Suddenly he looked at his watch again and said: 'But now we must go and see Mr Le Messurier.'

After her initial feeling of faintness on hearing Clive's report on the basement, Jennie had little stomach for further delving, but Clive's enthusiasm was irresistible and soon they were sitting in the Morris Minor, winding their way through the narrow streets in the centre of St Peter Port, bound for the house of Mr Le Messurier.

Chapter Twelve

Pedvin Road was an unprepossessing little back street of tiny, drab and down-at-heel terrace houses. Here lived Pierre Le Messurier, in a grey little house, in every respect like its two dozen shabby neighbours, except possibly for an even more evident air of decay. Post-war development had yet to reach Pedvin Road. And so it remained a steep, narrow defile, clogged with dogs and children at play, looking much the same as it had for two hundred years – a small scrap of Guernsey heritage within a stone's throw of the commercial heart of St Peter Port. It led steeply down the hillside to the market area of the town, its tortuous, twisting carriageway more suited to the horse and trap than to the motor car. Parking in the vicinity was impossible and for that reason, Jennie made her way to the sea front and there parked her car on one of the piers that surrounded the old harbour. Then she and Dumas began walking towards Pedvin Road, past the great grey granite building that housed the fish market.

During the drive from Bangalore, Dumas had started to fill in the background to the meeting that was about to take place. This he continued, as they walked towards Le Messurier's house.

First he explained that, having made up his mind that the most likely reason for the existence of a basement at Bangalore was the intention of establishing a headquarters for a German-sponsored clandestine group, either during or before the Occupation, he had begun ringing round all his old informants with a new set of questions. At first his efforts had been unrewarded, but very quickly he got the impression that some people knew very much more than they were prepared to admit. Indeed one or two clammed up completely with evident signs of guilt-laden terror. However, after considerable thick-skinned persistence and copious promises of confidentiality, one or two began to talk.

Dumas was warming to his subject. 'I'm sure you are aware that there was a strong element of mysticism in the upper echelons of the Nazi Party. Hitler's preoccupation with astrology has been well publicised. But it didn't end there. All his chosen leaders – well many of them anyway – seemed to share his liking for the occult, generally gingered up with huge chunks of racial mythology and a smattering of medieval fact. They took what they wanted out of the world's folk legends and myths and built a new culture for themselves one that suited their crazy ideology and would appeal to the weird tastes of their fanatical followers – whether German or quisling.

'You see, the Nazis were adept at borrowing folk traditions that held a special place in the hearts of the people they wanted to dominate, and using them for their own ends. Most countries have such traditions; a good example is the Icelandic sagas. These strange and blood-thirsty tales have an unnatural hold over many present-day Icelanders – quite wise and otherwise sane individuals, many of them; yet absolutely potty about Ulrich the Red, or some other chap with an equally unlikely name and superhuman abilities to match. These pillars of Icelandic society form associations, often secret or semi-secret, whose sole object seems to be to relive the sagas, to build reality out of myth. The Nazis did precisely the same thing with the legends of the Teutonic Knights. This was why Hitler was fascinated by the Wagner operas. They were mostly based on Teutonic legends – tapping a strong vein of folk tradition to which some people loved to cling in those uncertain, but materialistic, times. This isn't a solely foreign characteristic either, you know. We Brits do just the same with our legends of King Arthur and the Round Table, Robin Hood, and Hereward the Wake. Also just think of the Sealed Knot. Fully grown men playing at being soldiers in Cromwellian times.

'As an example of what I mean about Nazi mysticism, take Himmler's lair at Schloss Wewelsburg in Westphalia. Have you heard of it?'

Jennie shook her head. She could hardly believe what she was hearing. Reality had become intangible, as fleeting as thistledown, as insubstantial as ectoplasm. What she was now listening to could not be part of the world in which she wished to live. It could have nothing to do with her once-comfortable, uncomplicated home named Bangalore. With gathering momentum, a terrifying story seemed to be unfolding – a story which seemed to be engulfing her and one with which she did not wish to be associated.

Dumas continued: 'Well this medieval castle was rebuilt at enormous expense by Himmler and became the centre of his vile operations. In the heart of the *Schloss* was a large hall containing a huge table, surrounded by twelve chairs, one for each of Himmler's *Obergruppenführers,* or Knights of the Black Order of the SS. There was a throne there too, for Himmler himself – thirteen places in all, a witch's coven, you note. The Arthurian overtones, also, are quite plain. Here, in Schloss Wewelsburg this elitist group would take part in their own secret rituals, meditate on the future of the greater Reich and await divine guidance on how to achieve the Arian superstate, which was the Nazis' dream.

'But that wasn't all. Under this castle was a large mausoleum, known as the Realm of the Dead, in the centre of which was a sort of well, containing a stone vessel in which, when one of the knights died, his ashes were placed and the vessel enshrined in one of the niches, prepared for this purpose, in the massive walls of this underground structure. It is even rumoured that Hitler's final resting place was originally intended to be here, in the middle of this chamber, surrounded by his Nazi elite. Anyway, things didn't turn out that way. It was a pretty thought, though.'

There didn't seem anything pretty to Jennie about the drift of Clive's lecture. For her, a chill had entered into the spring sunshine. Dumas, however, ignoring her silence, forged on. 'So you see there was a strong link between the Nazi mythology and the underground – the subterranean. That is point number one. Point number two: the Channel Islands, as I'm sure you know, are great places for legends of the supernatural – ghosts and goblins and the like. The west-coast parishes of Guernsey are full of such tales, odd superstitions and weird practices. In many respects these are fascinating and it would be a pity to see so-called civilisation scrub them out; but some are plain evil, particularly when they encourage hatred of other social groups, or minorities, or simply people who don't hold similar views. Often such groups survive on an unhealthy diet of fear, hatred and secrecy. If such societies existed here, they would have been just what our Nazi friends were looking for to form the basis of a clandestine organisation.'

At that point in Clive's explanation, they had reached the door of No. 56 Pedvin Road. Its doorstep was embellished by two empty and badly rinsed milk bottles. Clive rang the bell. He just had time to add in a semi-whisper, 'Le Messurier, I am assured, is *the* expert on Guernsey folk legends', when the door opened and a thin-faced, rat-like man of around fifty appeared, looking at them with ill-disguised suspicion. Dumas introduced himself, and then

Jennie, simply as Mrs James and without further explanation.

'We spoke on the phone, you remember, Mr Le Messurier?'

Somewhat begrudgingly Le Messurier nodded and stood aside in silence, allowing them to pass into his house.

The front door opened directly into a tiny living room, filled with, what seemed to be, the accumulated rubbish of years – books; untidily folded newspapers; an ancient typewriter; a plate stained with egg yolk and carrying an egg-cup, complete with eggshell; mugs with the dried-on remains of coffee or tea; and an antique desk lamp with a cracked green glass shade. And everywhere there was paper – stacks of typescripts and manuscripts, all over-spread by layers of dust, which varied in thickness depending on how recently each pile had been rummaged through.

Le Messurier's mean little face was complemented by a thin, quarrelsome voice and an unfortunate habit of injecting into his sentences unnecessary and explosive little cries of 'eh' which cracked from his lips with the violence of distant rifle fire.

'Well,' he squeaked, 'what's all this about, eh? I can't see how I can help you. I'm a busy man. I haven't time to waste on tomfoolery. Why should I tell you anything anyway, eh?' So saying, he shut his lips so tightly that they almost disappeared into his face. His eyes, however, continued to stare belligerently at Dumas.

Jennie was so disconcerted by the man's rudeness that she was almost turning on her heel and leaving the depressing little room and its unpleasant occupant, when she was halted by Clive's opening words. These gave no sign of irritation at Le Messurier's attitude. Beaming at him, he said, 'There's absolutely no reason why you should spend your valuable time on us, Mr Le Messurier. So good of you to see us at all. We don't want to disturb you in your important work, but *you are* the leading authority on the folklore of the Islands. It would have been stupid of us to take our little problem to anyone less well qualified – impolite, even, to ignore your greater expertise. Clearly, if anyone can help us, it is you. And we know we can rely on the accuracy of anything you tell us.'

Jennie stared with wonder at Clive's face. It gave not the slightest hint that his words were anything but one hundred percent sincere. As for Le Messurier, he was totally taken in by Dumas's calculated flattery. He visibly swelled, puffing out his little chest and leaning back in his chair, the better to enjoy this adulation. At its conclusion, he waved his visitors towards two dining chairs with something approaching good will.

Once seated, Dumas continued, leaning encouragingly towards Le Messurier over his paper-strewn desk: 'You see, we have reason to believe that during the Occupation – maybe even before – the Germans were operating an undercover organisation on Guernsey; one that, maybe, was, as it were, grafted on to an existing secret Guernsey folk society – you know the sort of thing – secret rituals, witchcraft, the occult and the rest. What we were wondering was whether you have any knowledge of the existence of such a group, or groups in the 1930s.'

'Why do you want to know, eh?' The little man's tone was still cold, betraying not the least sign of friendship. Jennie could not dispel the feeling that she and Clive were wasting their time. 'You know as much as anyone about the Germans' activities during the Occupation, don't you?'

His compliment to Dumas was paid without the genuine, open-handed enthusiasm which Dumas had exuded. 'And what about her, eh?' Le Messurier asked, gesturing rudely towards Jennie.

'Mrs James has a special interest in the subject,' explained Dumas, accompanying this vague reply with one of his most winning smiles, 'and my knowledge of the Occupation, as you put it, does not include this type of thing. We're not talking about the usual Gestapo stuff. What we're looking for is – how shall I say? – much more specialised. Which is why we came to you.'

'Most odd,' was the only comment from Le Messurier, still staring at Dumas as though at something slightly distasteful. For a long time no one said anything. The house was silent, except for the puttering of a small gas fire, which was fighting a losing battle against the chill in the room. Outside, the dogs barked fitfully and the children shouted to each other, their running footsteps echoing between the terraces of houses.

At last Le Messurier spoke, 'What about the Templars then? Have you thought about them, eh?' It was impossible to tell whether, during his long silence, he had been genuinely seeking a solution to their problem, or simply making up his mind if he dared to impart this intriguing bit of information.

Dumas was clearly taken aback. 'The Templars? You mean the Knights Templar, the Poor Knights of Christ and of the Temple of Solomon, the military order of monks which was established at the time of the crusades?'

'Of course I do.'

'But on Guernsey? I never knew the Knights Templar had any connection with the Channel Islands,' replied Dumas.

'Where did they not have connection, I should like to know? And what happened to the Templars' fleet that disappeared from La Rochelle, eh – disappeared on the night the Order was disbanded? Scuttled at sea? Or hidden away in some friendly port?' There was another long pause, at the end of which Le Messurier had obviously decided that the interview was at an end. 'I will say no more. It's up to you now. Good day.'

'But are you telling me that there existed some organisation on the island in the twentieth century that owed its origins to an order of monks that was disbanded in the thirteenth or fourteenth century?'

'I will say no more,' Le Messurier repeated. 'Good day.'

So saying, he turned his back on his visitors and began laboriously punching the keys of his typewriter. Jenny and Clive grimaced at each other and left, murmuring thanks which neither felt Le Messurier had deserved and which the little man, at any rate, ignored.

*

That afternoon the weather, which in the morning had been so promising, began to deteriorate. By evening it had become wicked. A wind sprang up, lashing the trees along the cliff edge and howling eerily about the bungalow. After a snack lunch in one of the harbour-side bars, Jennie had returned to Bangalore, whilst Clive Dumas had sought the assistance of the St Peter Port librarian.

Neither he nor Jennie felt the interview with Le Messurier had been fruitful; yet there was something significant, Dumas felt, in his obvious reluctance to mention the Templars.

'I feel he just couldn't resist dropping out that tease about the Templars,' he explained to Jennie, 'probably against his better judgement, I guess; but having let the cat out of the bag, he was too timid to go any further. That sort of little man can rarely resist the temptation to display his knowledge. Anyway, it was a useful hint which I can follow up this afternoon. I want to pay a visit to my old friend, Fred Guilbert – the librarian, you know. He's a mine of information on local history – and very much more congenial company than our friend of this morning. He might be able to throw some light on the Templar business too.' Dumas laughed. 'What a little prig, Le Messurier turned out to be – and unless I'm very much mistaken, a scared little prig into the bargain.'

Jennie and Clive had parted on the sea front, as the rising wind plucked at the usually smooth waters of the inner harbour, turning them peevishly choppy. Once more alone, driving back to the bungalow, Jennie had realised that her light-heartedness of the morning had been shattered by the events of the day. Now she was once more suffering from that dull ache of unhappiness that had been, to a greater or lesser extent, her constant companion for several months. Now, however, her unhappiness had been tainted by fear.

When Dumas returned by taxi to Bangalore that evening, he was full of confidence and good humour. He plunged from the car to the front door through the fitful squalls of rain, clearly bursting to tell Jennie of his news. 'I've spent a most rewarding afternoon,' he told her. 'Fred Guilbert really is a magician. If there is a rabbit to be dragged out of a hat, Fred's the man to do it. I'll have to go back to the library tomorrow morning to complete my crash course on the Knights Templar, but I do believe we may be on to something.'

Jennie sighed. 'Oh, Clive, I don't know. I'm so confused. Why are we doing all this? I've been asking myself this question all afternoon – why, why, why? – and I just don't reach any sort of answer. Everything I learn about Bangalore makes me more unhappy. It's horrible. I wish I'd never begun all this. I wish I'd never discovered the rotten basement. Then I wouldn't have started this stupid enquiry – prying into things best left alone.' She paused, seeing the sudden disappointment on Clive's face.

'Oh hell, I'm sorry, Clive. I sound so ungrateful, don't I? You've been so helpful, wasted so much of your valuable time on my silly problems. Please don't think I'm not grateful, but can you understand what I mean? Ever since I started asking questions, things have been going wrong. First there was poor Mr Johnson—'

'Your poor Mr Johnson,' Dumas interrupted, 'probably had a lot more to answer for than you think. If I were you, I wouldn't waste your sympathy on him.'

'But that wasn't the end of it. All my feelings about this place have been ruined. Everything's turning me against Bangalore, and to think, when I bought it, and for the first few months here, I was convinced it was the nearest thing to paradise on earth that I could ever find.'

Clive Dumas, suddenly subdued, took off his raincoat in silence and followed Jennie into the lounge. Here he watched her, pouring two pre-dinner gin and tonics. What he saw was a sad, middle-aged woman with lines of pain and loss inscribed on her face. When Jennie had first come to Guernsey, before Clive knew her, those lines had been cut deeply by the shock of the sudden death of her husband and all her subsequent worries. The effect of the first months on the island, however, had begun to smooth them away. Now they had returned, etched even more deeply. For the first time, Clive wondered if he was being fair to her. How much was the research now driven by his own curiosity, rather than by Jennie's need?

'I'm sorry, Clive,' said Jennie, handing him his drink. 'I think all this has been brought on by that horrid little man this morning.'

'Yes; he was pretty odious, wasn't he?'

Jennie shuddered. 'I don't know why I let it worry me. What does it matter anyway? But everything about this wretched basement seems to have sinister overtones.'

'Seriously, Jennie, it's for you to decide. I don't want to interfere. I would only say one thing: now you know about the existence of the basement, you can never pretend it isn't there. You can't turn the clock back. Maybe knowing the truth is better than allowing your fantasies to build up, uncontrolled by reality.'

Jennie prowled about the room, looking ill at ease. She had heard that advice before. She recalled the words of the rector of St Saviour's: 'Imagined problems are usually worse than the real thing... I don't suppose there is any going back now.' What should she do? She found it impossible to make a decision. 'I don't know; I really do not know,' was all she said.

'I tell you what,' cried Dumas, suddenly brightening. 'Do you play Scrabble, Jennie?'

She nodded.

'I was sure you would. Tonight there's going to be no more talk about the basement. We'll eat your delicious dinner, Jennie, and then I'll take you on at Scrabble. How about that?'

'How do you know the meal's going to be delicious?'

'Could it be anything else?'

She smiled. 'All right; Scrabble it is; but I'm not sure that we are equally matched. Poor me against the established author!'

They passed a pleasant evening, each carefully avoiding any reference to Jennie's problems. Only as they bade goodnight, did Clive Dumas mention his plans for the next day.

'Look here, about tomorrow; I've organised for the taxi to pick me up at eight-thirty. Don't let me disturb you, I never eat breakfast anyway. I'll just get a coffee in St Peter Port before I go to the library, so you don't need to worry about me in the morning. I'll be busy in the library until about midday, after that I'll go to the same bar where we were at lunchtime today. You think about what you want to do. If you decide to continue with the investigation, meet me in the bar at about twelve-thirty and I'll buy you a beer and a sandwich. If you're not there, I'll not trouble you again – unless you call me. I quite understand your feelings and I don't want to make things worse for you, I really don't. I'm booked on the afternoon flight back to Alderney.' He smiled at her. Gently he leaned forward and kissed her. 'Goodnight, and thank you for a wonderful dinner and an enjoyable evening. I haven't had such fun for years.'

With that, Clive Dumas retired, leaving Jennie sitting thoughtfully beside her great granite fireplace.

Chapter Thirteen

Preparing for bed, Jennie was comforted by the thought that Clive Dumas was sleeping in the next room. At least she was no longer alone – mentally adrift. Now she had the companionship of a real living friend; and one with whom she enjoyed a unique rapport. He understood her dilemma and she was confident that he would be able to provide her with the support she so badly needed.

Unfortunately, once more, her relief was short-lived. Immediately she drifted into sleep, she was beset by a succession of nightmare vignettes, which made their appearance like rocks in a shallow and turbulent sea. They flashed into her sleeping mind, nonsensically, without relevance to anything in her experience and with no thread of continuity running between them. As quickly as they appeared, they disappeared leaving her tossing in a troubled wakefulness, until the next rock thrust itself through the dark waters of that night. Dawn had started to lighten the eastern sky before Jennie plunged into a truly deep sleep, and with this came a dream more bewildering and terrible than any she had experienced so far in Mrs Grace's 'dear bed'. This dream carried her far from Bangalore; far, too, from Guernsey, to a time and place beyond her wildest imaginings – to an incident packed with medieval barbarity.

Yet it was all frighteningly familiar – the brutal events she was condemned to watch – as though she had witnessed them all before and then had locked them away in the labyrinths of her subconscious, from where nothing escapes. They were too horrifying to let roam free; but now, centuries later, the time had come for them to be recalled to her conscious mind in all their ghastly detail. The weft of time, reacting to some supernatural command, had bulged and allowed a fragment of the past to escape.

In the dream, all her senses were acutely tuned to the spectacle, of which she was the unwilling observer. She saw the moonlight reflecting off the waters of a mighty river in which lay a tiny islet where the spectacle was to be performed. Her nose was irritated by the cloying smell of wood smoke, tainted by the stench of burning animal fat that had been poured on the logs to make them flame more fiercely. Her ears echoed with the ghostly chanting of the priests, rising over the sub-human growling of the mob of spectators that lined both river banks. She was about to witness a ceremony of regal vengeance, acted out in the name of religious justice.

It all started with mist, swirling, blinding, engulfing. And as the mists cleared, a grotesque procession emerged from the shadows, in the centre of which limped two feeble old men. They were dressed in simple white smocks, each emblazoned with a bold cross of red on its breast. Surrounding these men were an assortment of others – soldiers, clerics and royal officials. First came the officials in sumptuous robes, then the guards shepherding their two aged prisoners, then two priests, clad in ecclesiastical splendour and with hands clasped in an attitude of prayer. Painfully the old men, each accompanied by a priest, made their way up the small slope towards the centre of the islet, where two large piles of brushwood and faggots had been placed around two stout stakes. The old men walked with difficulty, as though their legs had become unused to movement, maybe after long years of incarceration. Around them marched their guards, seven in number, kitted out in chain mail and armed with broad swords and pikes. Their presence, though, was mere conven-

tion – just for show. There was little need for such a force to prevent the escape of these feeble and pitiful old men. Their time was already spent. They simply awaited the final indignity that was about to be inflicted upon them – a degrading death by public execution.

The entourage passed through the ring of Royal Guards, standing shoulder to shoulder surrounding the execution site. It approached the two innocent-seeming piles of debris at the very centre of the islet. One old man was led to each pile and forced to climb to the stake at its summit, helped along by thrusts from the guards' pikes. Their progress was infinitely slow. They slipped and staggered, pitching about on the loose brushwood like ships on a rough sea. Continually they tripped and were forced to struggle to their feet again to the huge amusement of the mob on the distant river banks. Outside the ring of guards on the islet stood other observers, a select group, remote from the mob and enjoying a privileged vantage point. These were clearly royal officials in full regalia, summoned there to witness that justice (of a sort) was done. Unlike the mob, these remained silent, unmoved by the events before them.

Time passed. It seemed that the old men would never succeed in making the ascent; and then the younger of the two (but still a man well into his seventh decade) fell. He had been within an ace of reaching the stake, and now lay, barely conscious, at the foot of the pile. When he was dragged to his feet by one of the guards, blood was flowing from a huge gash on the side of his face. The mob screamed with delight and even the special observers on the islet could be seen to be appreciating the display. At last the two prisoners were manhandled by the guards to their assigned positions at the stakes and there they were bound – the younger with his hands tied together behind the stake, the elder, at his own request, with his hands tied together before him in an attitude of prayer, his body lashed to the stake. The two priests began chanting and two young guards withdrew flaming brands from a small fire, close by, and thrust them into the dry straw at the base of each bonfire. The distant mob went insane with delight.

Just as the flames were about to reach the younger man, he screamed and then with a supreme effort of will, restrained all further audible demonstration of his agony. His face was contorted by the effort. As for the older man, he remained silent, as though in prayer, until the flames were lapping at his feet and then he spoke. Even though his voice was ancient and thin, it carried to the privileged spectators. It even carried across the water to the mob on the river banks, who fell silent in order to hear the old man's words. He declaimed his short speech as though giving a sermon to a restless and inattentive congregation – and his words were terrible and charged with fury. Even the continued chanting of the priests could not drown them. When he was finished, the mists returned and the fearful spectacle was obliterated.

In Jennie's mind, her own screams matched the torment of the prisoners, who she seemed to know, yet did not know. Image by image she recognised the event as a part of her past, but no part of her remembered past. How could it be? And as she fought her way out of the depths of sleep; she seemed to be screaming in the victims' voices – crying in their agony.

Chapter Fourteen

At about midday, Jennie was sitting in the harbour bar at a table near the window. Outside, the sea front, swept by rain squalls, wore its out-of-season look, populated by a bevy of squealing gulls, a few parked cars and even fewer pedestrians. In the harbour the masts of a fleet of untenanted yachts bobbed to the swell and waited patiently for the return of their owners, fair-weather sailors to a man.

Jennie was feeling drained. All night she had been tossing in a fitful, shallow and disturbingly troubled sleep. Only towards dawn had she eventually plunged into a truly deep unconsciousness, and a dream so vivid that it swept her to a land she did not know and a time that was buried in antiquity – a time of violence and of savage revenge – a time of evil performed in the name of true religion. By the time she had woken, Clive Dumas had long since left for the library. All she had for company was the Bangalore sound, which that morning seemed to her to be shrieking, like a pack of malevolent banshees.

A furious struggle raged within her. Should she, or should she not, keep her lunchtime rendezvous in St Peter Port with Clive? All morning she mooned about the bungalow, on the face of it wracked with indecision, yet resigned in the unadmitted depths of her mind to the fact that, come midday, she would be sitting in the bar, looking out at the rain-sodden sea front and the argumentative gulls. She knew she had no choice, but to wait, resignedly, for the next act in her unimaginable drama.

Above all, whatever was to transpire, she had a compelling need to relate her dream to someone – to off-load some of the misery that it had left behind. If she didn't, she feared she might lose her reason. And who was there to tell, but Clive Dumas? How could she speak to anyone else – involve another person in the incomprehensible web within which she was ravelled?

All morning her dream had rested like a leaden weight upon her spirits. She was sure it carried huge significance, but what that significance was and how it meshed with her Bangalore dreams, escaped her. Nevertheless she was slowly grasping the fact that the mystery of Bangalore was governed by unexpected dimensions of time and space. She saw it no longer as a cosy little domestic mystery; but a huge saga beside which she was as nothing, dwarfed by the scale of the horror. From this point there could be no going back, no withdrawing from the story. It was not her will that was the driving force, but an unseen and undefined power that was pressing her onwards and would continue to do so, until whatever preordained outcome had been reached.

As she sat in the bar, she was so absorbed with her own thoughts, that she did not immediately notice Clive enter. He was almost at her side before she looked up and saw him. His face clearly registered the pleasure – relief almost – that he felt on seeing that she had decided to keep the rendezvous. She, too, sensed a lightening in the day. Their eyes met; their mutual complicity was cemented.

'So pleased you're here. What can I get you to eat and drink?' he asked.

Seated with their drinks and waiting for their food to be served, they both hesitated to open the subject that was uppermost in their minds. Dumas read the weariness and worry in Jennie's face and, for a moment, doubted whether her decision was to advance, or to retreat. Even while he hesitated, Jennie began to speak. As she did so, her eyes ranged sightlessly about the sea front, avoiding Clive's gaze.

'Last night – no, it was this morning, quite late – that's why I didn't wake up in time to see you off – I had a dream. You must hear about it – now, before we talk about anything else. If I don't tell you, I think I'll go crazy. It was so vivid – it still is, there, inside my head and yet at the same time it was so gruesomely unreal. I can't describe the feeling of horror that it's left me with. It was like being right inside a painting by... oh, which of the old masters was it? The one who specialised in huge canvases, full of people, depicting grotesque, bloodthirsty events – hell even...'

'Hieronymus Bosch,' Clive suggested.

'That's it; that's who I mean,' cried Jennie, 'and I was right there; right inside this ghoulish fantasy. But it was no fantasy. It was terribly, terribly real.'

Jennie paused and took a sip from her glass.

'There was this island, quite a small island really; not in the sea, you understand, but in the centre of a huge river. There were boats drawn up on its shore and people, lots of people, standing on the river bank watching what was happening on the island. There was another small group of onlookers on the island itself, but they were obviously a bit special, all dressed in old-fashioned, expensive robes. The thing, which was so strange about them, was their complete silence. It was as though everyone was waiting for something to happen. There were soldiers there too, with swords and pikes. They were drawn up to form a great ring round the high ground in the centre of the island. They stood, shoulder to shoulder, with their backs to the high ground, facing the spectators. Yes, there was another strange thing too; all the spectators were men. I didn't see any women there at all.

'On the high ground, there were two piles of faggots and brushwood with a great stake sticking out of the centre of each one. Suddenly I realised that what I was looking at was an execution site and the piles of brushwood were bonfires, on which two people were to be burned alive. Suddenly the silence of the crowd on the river banks was broken by an excited murmur, like the buzzing of angry insects, and two men – old men – were led out by guards and taken, one to each bonfire. As they were forced to climb on to these piles of brushwood, urged on by their guards, who prodded at them with their pikes, the buzzing in the crowd gave way to a vicious snarl, punctuated by yelps of laughter as the old men stumbled and lurched from side to side on the loose logs, as though they were drunk, and the crowd jeered at them, taunting them. One old man fell and when he stood up again, blood was streaming down his face. This made the crowd whoop and scream with delight. At last both prisoners were on top of the bonfires and there they were secured to the stakes. The younger man's arms were forced behind the stake and tied together. The other one argued with his guards about this and eventually they tied the ropes around his body, leaving his bound hands before him; so that he could pray, I should think. The expression on their faces was heart-rending – I can't begin to describe it – but the oldest man showed no fear, only a deep, despairing disappointment. Both men were dressed in a kind of uniform, just a plain white smock with a huge red cross on the front.

'As I watched, two men with flaming brands set light to the bonfires and the two priests, one beside each fire, began to chant prayers. As for the men on the river banks, they seemed to go mad with excitement, shouting, screaming, leaping up and down and hurling abuse at the prisoners. It was unspeakable.'

Jennie paused, as though gathering her strength for the next part of her story. Clive remained silent, his eyes fixed on Jennie's pale face.

'As the flames leaped higher, the older man began to make a speech. He declaimed the words in a terrible voice which betrayed no hint of fear. I couldn't tell what he was saying – I guess it was in old-fashioned French, but I'm not sure. His voice was incredibly thin and feeble, yet at the same time so clear and angry that I'm sure everyone there, who could understand the language, must have heard every word, even though the priests chanted louder to try to drown what he was saying. The other man – the one with the bleeding face – screamed once as the flames reached him. Then he remained silent, his face contorted with the effort to stifle any further screams of agony. As for the older man, he continued to speak, despite the flames, which by then had ignited his smock and his voice gave no hint of the agony he must have been feeling. When he had finished his speech, the flames and smoke billowed upwards, obscuring the scene. It was as though they had been ordered to finish their evil work quickly. Yet still the echoes of the old man's voice seemed to be rebounding off the river banks.'

There was a long pause, and then Jennie said in a tiny, weary voice: 'That's all I saw.'

'It's incredible,' exclaimed Clive Dumas, 'truly incredible.'

'Horrible.'

'That too, but unbelievably accurate. That's the important thing,' insisted Dumas, 'its accuracy. You have just related an event that I have read about for the first time today. Does the name of Jacques de Molay mean anything to you?'

Jennie shook her head.

'Well he was (according to the official history anyway) the last Grand Master of the Knights Templar. I believe that you've just described his execution, which took place on an island in the middle of the River Seine in 1314. Isn't that incredible? If it is so, it certainly seems to confirm a link with the Knights Templar. Maybe Le Messurier was right after all.'

'How do you mean, the link with the Templars?' Jennie asked. 'Do you mean that because I dreamed about this execution, it's got to have some connection with Bangalore? Couldn't it just be coincidence, or maybe that I had heard the story years ago and simply forgotten about it, although it remained lurking in my subconscious – then, because we were talking about the Templars yesterday, it struggled up to the surface again?' Jennie was clutching at straws, and she knew it.

Dumas was not impressed. 'All your special dreams have had some relevance to the past of the bungalow, haven't they?' he insisted. 'So why not this? Let me tell you a bit more about the end of the Order of the Knights Templar and then see what you think.'

Dumas rummaged in his bag and took out his notebook, to which he referred from time to time as he spoke.

'The Order was effectively dissolved in France on – let me see – 13th October, 1307 – a Friday, incidentally; some say that's where the superstition about Friday 13th comes from. This was when the then King of France, Philippe IV, commanded the arrest of every member of the Order in his kingdom. At the same time, Pope Clement V, who in this was acting very much as the French king's lackey, issued a papal bull to all other European rulers instructing them to act similarly. Some did; some ignored the command. Philippe, however, was the chief initiator of the destruction of the Templars. He organised the arrests to take place at dawn on 13th October and almost immediately many of the imprisoned knights were tortured, charged with a number of crimes; secular, spiritual and sexual; the chief among which was heresy. If the Order were found guilty of just this one crime of heresy, that would have been sufficient for its wealth in land, property and gold to be forfeit to the Crown. This was Philippe's objective, being not only jealous of the power of the Order, but also strapped for cash at the time.

'I don't know if you know much about the Templars, but in a nutshell the Order was originally founded after the First Crusade in 1118 to act as an international body of military monks, bound by vows of chastity, poverty and unquestioning obedience to its Grand Master. Their job was to guard the pilgrims en route to the Holy Land and live and die in the defence of the True Cross. Gradually the wealth and influence of the Order, which owed no allegiance to any other authority, but the Pope, increased until it was the envy of all the royal families in Europe. In fact, eventually, the Order started to act as a sort of banker to the royalty – and you know how wealthy bankers can become!

'Well, on the appointed day, the king's men swooped on the Templars' strongholds, which were scattered throughout France – throughout the whole of Europe, come to that. Philippe's men imprisoned all the knights they could find and impounded all the Order's property. The Inquisition took over the job of exacting confessions from each and every one of the members of the Order. The brutality was unimaginable. You mentioned Hieronymus Bosch. Well, this was real-life Hieronymus Bosch! Those that confessed were imprisoned and, having served their time, were freed; those that maintained their innocence or withdrew their confessions were executed in the most brutal fashion.

'Right at the end of this blood-letting came the Grand Master and his lieutenant, de Charney. In their case, the authorities made rather a cock up of it. They thought that, after months of ill-treatment at the hands of the Inquisition, Jacques de Molay and other leaders of the sect were in a mood to confess. So they laid on a great public spectacle on the steps of Notre Dame in the centre of Paris early in the morning of 18th March, 1314, at which de Molay was publicly to confess his sins and those of the Order.

'The whole charade was designed to justify to the public at large the bestial way in which the Order had been put down. Well, de Molay, instead of confessing, launched into a stinging attack upon Philippe and declared the innocence of himself and his Order. De Charney followed suit. The soldiers stepped in and both recalcitrants were hustled away as quickly as possible to minimise the loss of face, King Philippe clearly suffered. He, the King, had a real dilemma on his hands. He wasn't sure of the effect of this debacle on the sentiments of the people of Paris and so he decided to defuse what he saw as a potentially inflammable situation. He ordered the immediate execution of the prisoners, not in the centre of Paris, which might have incited a riot, but on an island in the Seine, away from public interference. The ceremony was watched by a relatively small gathering of Philippe's loyal supporters. However, as you saw in your dream, the public got to know of the burnings and watched from the river banks.'

Whilst Clive had been speaking the two ham salads, which he had ordered when he bought the drinks at the bar, had been brought to their table. There they lay, still untouched.

'How extraordinary,' murmured Jennie. She automatically took up a knife and fork and began to eat in an absent-minded way. 'But how could these events over six hundred years ago be linked to Guernsey today; and even more particularly, to Bangalore?'

Clive, who was also starting to eat, continued his story between mouthfuls. 'You noticed I said *most* of the knights were imprisoned on that fateful Friday 13th, not *all*. However well planned and efficient the dawn swoop of Philippe's army, a few knights slipped through their fingers. No one knows how many. I told you that some European leaders ignored the papal bull; notable among these was the King of Spain. Many Templars must have slipped across the Pyrenees and joined the Spanish Templars. Some disappeared into Germany, where tales of their continued existence became mixed up with the legends of the Teutonic Knights. Some joined the rival military monks, the Knights of the Order of the Hospital of St John of Jerusalem – the Hospitallers, as they are often called. Incidentally this Order continued in existence for many centuries. It was even responsible for the founding of the St John's Ambulance Brigade. And do you remember what Le Messurier said about the missing Templar fleet, slipping away from La Rochelle? No one is really sure where the fleet went; but might it not have taken refuge on an offshore island, owned at the time by the Duke of Normandy, who was often on extremely poor terms with the King of France?'

'It all starts to make sense,' exclaimed Jennie.

'It does indeed, and the extra information Fred Guilbert was able to give me, makes it look even more sure that we have arrived at the truth at last – if we want to know the truth, that is.' With these words Clive Dumas peered uncertainly at Jennie, betraying his deep concern – a concern which had been growing, as he had told his story. After hearing Jennie's latest dream, he could not avoid drawing uncanny, frightening conclusions that made the future seem unsure and threatening. Gone from his face was the recent look of boyish excitement. Carefree enthusiasm had been replaced by worry and uncertainty. For the first time he was admitting the real possibility that Jennie might be in physical danger.

Jennie made no reply. They finished their meal in silence, heads bowed together over their plates like two conspirators. Then they left the bar.

'Let me drive you to the airport,' Jennie offered, as they crossed the road outside the bar.

Dumas appeared unsure. 'Thanks, that would be very kind, but I don't want to be a nuisance. I've already taken up too much of your time. But then again, I haven't quite finished my story yet, and if you really want to pursue the mystery, I think you should know all the facts. I suppose knowledge is a good thing. That way you are forearmed; although the truth may disturb you. Unfortunately, I must be back on Alderney tonight. I have a meeting with the States about my next alterations at Colombé. This is a pity – for all sorts of reasons. Mainly because I feel now is the wrong time to leave you to cope with this problem on your own; but I'm afraid I've no alternative.'

'Come on, we can talk on the way,' replied Jennie as she unlocked the car. 'As far as I can see, I have no choice. I must carry on with my search now. It's not down to me any longer.'

Dumas nodded. 'I think you're right. Okay, well here goes. During their official existence, the Templars were excessively secretive. That was at once their strength and their undoing. Secrecy begets suspicion – often unnecessary suspicion. Think of the effects that the secrecy shrouding present-day Freemasonry has had on the public's perception of that movement. Nevertheless secrecy has a strengthening effect as well, binding a society's adherents together more closely – making them feel privileged members of an exclusive club. Since the Order's dissolution, rumours have been circulating throughout much of Western Europe about secret groups of Templars still operating in all sorts of fields; some legal, some illegal. This is particularly true of areas of Europe under the German sphere of influence. Now, no doubt, you start to see the drift of the argument?'

'Only too clearly,' Jennie replied glumly.

'Fred Guilbert believes that some such secret society, claiming ancestry stretching back to the Templars, was in existence on Guernsey before the war. Whilst the story of the Templar fleet might or might not be true, it seems unlikely to him that there really was a genetic line stretching from the genuine Templars to the pre-war club. For one thing, the Templars would have had to give up their vow of celibacy, if any sort of heritage line was to be created – but stranger things have happened.' Dumas gave a wry smile.

'Anyway, a secret society does seem to have existed and two of its leading lights seem to have been Mr Johnson and Charles Grace. How the latter, as a non-islander, gained acceptance into an islanders' secret society, no one knows. It suggests unnatural influence – or some special qualification in one of the international affiliates. Fred believes Grace had already been enrolled by the Germans before he came to the island – during his colonial service, in fact. When he arrived on the island, his connections (German or non-German) made him acceptable to this secret Guernsey group, which probably was already in effect a German clandestine organisation. Fred believes that many people during the Occupation knew – or at least had a fairly strong suspicion – that there existed an elite group of islanders who received special treatment from the Germans. There were differing opinions, however, as to why this was so. Fred, however, is in no doubt.

'Johnson was one of the Guernsey males who seemed to enjoy very special treatment from the Germans. He made a lot of money during the war, commandeering empty property left by the departed British islanders, fleeing before the arrival of the Germans. After the war there was a lot of money to be made out of this property, much of which was never claimed by its true owners at the end of the conflict, surprising as it may seem. No; Johnson did a grand job of feathering his own nest. A typical example of being in the right place at the right time and having friends in both camps. When the Germans came, Charles Grace, being British, had to make it appear that he had left the island. (All mainland males were automatically interned by the Germans, you see; an exception in his case would have caused comment.) Apparently, though, he didn't leave the island, or if he did, he came back as a protégé of the Germans – and, presumably, leader of this clandestine group that now found itself directly controlled by the Germans. Maybe Charles Grace had been singled out to act as the intermediary between the German Clandestines and an English clandestine group on the mainland. Who can tell? All that is certain is that he disappeared during the war and was never seen again. Mrs Grace returned after the war, I would imagine, to make sure there was no incriminating evidence left in Bangalore, and to sell the property – at an attractive price – to a sad widow from the mainland, who would not know (or care) about the rumours that existed on the island. How about that? Neat, isn't it?'

As Dumas finished this story, they drove into the car park of the airport. They were early for the Alderney flight, and so, for a time, sat in the car, looking at the rain-sodden turf.

'I just don't know what to say,' said Jenny, 'what to say, or what to think – and most of all, what to do.'

Dumas regarded her narrowly for an instant, and then said, 'There is one last snippet of information – and this could be the most worrying of all. It depends on what belief you have in things supernatural. I've never been a great one for the occult myself, but I'm bound to admit some of the aspects of this case make me have doubts about my scepticism.'

Jennie didn't turn her head, only her lips moved: 'Go on, Clive. You can't stop now.'

'Everything I have told you so far has been fact, or intelligent speculation based on fact. Now for the legend. You know you said that, in your dream, the older man was making a speech as he was being burned? Well, rumour has it that just before he died, de Molay cursed King Philippe IV and Pope Clement V, challenging them both to meet him before the throne of God within one year to answer for their crimes against the Templars. In fact, Clement died within a month of the curse and Philippe about seven months later.'

Jennie gave an explosive shudder, as she listened to Dumas's words. Her eyes stared sightlessly at the rain on the windscreen.

He continued, 'Since then there have been endless stories of the curse of de Molay falling on all those who interfered with surviving groups of Templars. Indeed quite a cult of de Molay worship grew up and the night after the execution, many of the poor people of Paris swam across the river to sift through the ashes, looking for scraps of his bones, which had escaped the flames. That began a flourishing trade in de Molay relics – most of them, no doubt, fake. But the de Molay curse is said still to protect holders of genuine relics.

'Whether the Guernsey clandestine group held a genuine de Molay relic, or not, can only be the subject of speculation; but if they did, it could account for the apparent high level of paranormal activity that seems to surround Bangalore. Your attitude will depend on how much you believe in these things.

'Well, there you have it – the sum total of my researches. I can't make any comments; I'm still trying to make sense of it all in my own mind. I'm also suffering from mental indigestion, I think.'

Clive Dumas looked at his watch. 'I ought to go. I hate to leave you with all this to cope with. We must keep in touch. I'll ring you tomorrow to make sure everything's all right. Thanks for the hospitality. I'm sure we'll meet again – soon.' He leaned across to Jennie and kissed her lightly on her cheek. Then he was running through the rain towards the terminal building.

Half an hour later the Alderney flight rumbled along the runway and took off. Out of a window Dumas saw Jennie's Morris Minor still standing where he had left it, Jennie, behind the wheel, a thoughtful, shapeless form that didn't even wave.

Chapter Fifteen

'I think the woman's gone stark, raving mad,' exclaimed John Frensham, throwing down Jennie's latest letter amongst the chaos of his breakfast table. 'Loony as a coot! What a shame she had to go like that; such a nice girl in the old days. But I could see it coming. No mistaking the signs of instability. I had them spotted, plain as day, when I stayed with her last autumn.'

For all his cold and uncompromising words, John suffered from a niggling feeling of responsibility. He had recovered from the disappointment of realising that, whenever they spent time together, they were persistently irritating each other. That was no basis for a more permanent relationship, he told himself. And he accepted the truth of that fact. He was no longer the sort of man who would moon around after a woman, when she was evidently not temperamentally suited to him. And yet... and yet...

He lifted up the letter again, the first to arrive after many weeks of silence. He reread a section that, on first reading, had particularly intrigued him:

You see, John, ever since I found the basement and was unable to discover who put it there and for what purpose, I've become very ill at ease. At first I blamed you and your departure just before Christmas. I told myself it was maybe that that had unsettled me. Then I blamed the winter weather –

we get so much mild and murky weather here on Guernsey. It can be depressing. But now the nights are drawing out, the weather's getting better and I still feel bitterly, bitterly troubled.

Do you remember how you said you felt uneasy at Bangalore? Well now I feel exactly the same. I suppose it was the death of Mr Johnson, too, that unnerved me – and the fact that he was so evidently hiding something from me about the basement. Anyway, I couldn't let it rest and I got in touch with the author, Clive Dumas – he's an expert on the German Occupation, and the basement did seem to have something to do with the Germans. Well, he's been extremely helpful, trying to get to the bottom of this business. But ever since he's been involved, the bungalow seems to have turned against me – become positively malicious at times. I really don't think I can stay here, if it goes on like this. I dream so much and I feel so alone.

'Poor Jennie; quite, quite potty,' exclaimed John again, 'and now mixed up with a long-haired author chappie, too. I must give her a ring and see what's behind it all.'

That evening, when the cheap rate started, John tried to ring Bangalore, the ringing tone sounded repeatedly, but there was no reply.

'Maybe she's off gadding,' thought John, and – for a while at least – forgot all about Jennie and her problems.

It was three days later that John Frensham thought of Jennie again and tried once more to ring her. This time the call was intercepted by a recorded announcement, which informed him that the number was out of commission.

'What the hell do they mean by that?' he grumbled. 'Out of order, number changed, or has the silly woman just forgotten to pay her telephone bill?'

He rang up directory enquiries and was told there was no current record of a number for a Mrs Jennie James on the St Peter Port exchange. John was surprised, but not unduly worried. 'Potty woman,' he said, and started to make plans for the coming year's herbaceous borders in his so conventional Guildford garden.

★

For half-an-hour after Clive's plane took off, Jennie had remained seated in her car, her mind in turmoil. What should she do? The last thirty-six hours had turned her life upside down. She had learnt so much, experienced so much; she felt she needed a period in which to digest this surfeit of fact and speculation. And what did it all mean to her? How was it all to affect her and her relationship with Bangalore?

Suddenly she found that she was admitting to herself for the first time that she was afraid – afraid of her isolation in what she had believed was her own personal paradise, her bungalow, Bangalore. Her newly acquired knowledge certainly threatened her continuing life there. It also seemed to deny her the protection that she once had believed the insubstantial presence of Charles Grace ensured her. There even seemed to be doubt now about his loyalty during the war. Yet she could not believe he was capable of treachery, although it seemed the only logical conclusion. But if it were so, how did this accord with her dream of his execution by the Germans? She felt a cold dread of sleeping in Bangalore again, after the terrible implications of the previous night's dream. To sleep there once more might reveal even more facts she did not wish to know. But what could she do? Where could she go to escape? Book into a hotel? But that seemed so nonsensical – so easy, but so melodramatic. Anyway, what would it solve? Nothing. It would simply make the eventual return to Bangalore more difficult. She must not let her imagination dominate her life. Yet was it her imagination, or something more powerful?

During Clive's visit, she had become more and more convinced that, as far as Bangalore was concerned, her free will had been superseded by some external force. Looking back, she now realised that this force had been manipulating her life for a very long time, maybe even from her first day at Bangalore. In the beginning it had seemed seductively benign, but as time passed it had become increasingly malignant.

'But why me?' Jennie cried out in anguish. 'Why have I been chosen to delve through these unhappy events, to find a truth that does not concern me and is in every way repugnant? Or is it the fate of anyone who becomes the owner of Bangalore?' How could she know?

In the light of all that had been discovered during the past few days, it seemed possible that the least likely explanation for the origin of the Bangalore basement – that it had been secretly constructed at the time the bungalow was built – was the preferred option. If this were so, its purpose clearly was to provide a permanent home for a long-established Guernsey Templar society. And for this feat to have been accomplished, when its existence was omitted from the official building plans, implied the complicity of the builders, the States building inspectors and several other States officials. The Templar society obviously had powerful friends. Equally, it confirmed what Jennie had always suspected; that Mr Johnson had been lying, when she consulted him after discovering the basement.

As she sat in the car, it seemed to Jennie that everyone had been a party to the deception, even her dream companion, Charles Grace. At first he had been comforting and protective. But it had been he, who had started off the whole train of events which had led to her slide into this misery. Now his presence was no longer comforting. She had come to fear his next appearance. Who could she trust? Image after image passed through her mind, building up a maelstrom of thought and fantasy, until the one blended with the other and she had to grasp the steering wheel to stop herself from screaming. Her head fell forward on to her hands, and thus she stayed, until her racing thoughts calmed.

Suddenly she became conscious of a man watching her from a neighbouring car. Feeling embarrassed, she turned the key in the ignition and drove slowly out of the car park. Where should she go? Where else, but back to Bangalore? There seemed no alternative.

Chapter Sixteen

She felt the implacable drag of the tide upon her body – the sort of force that the flow of a mighty river exerts, powered at its source by melting mountain snows and sucked out of the land by gravity and the invisible magnetism of the moon. It was a force, at once helpful and untrustworthy, for it swept her towards her destination, yet always threatened to thrust the unwary swimmer beyond the desired landfall, too far downstream. She knew that her landfall needed to be accurate, well-timed and silent as the grave. And so she swam, using a strong breaststroke, arms and legs working well below the surface of the water so as to make no noise, thrusting herself across the current towards the small lump of rock in midstream. She had joined the river high upstream to avoid the soldiers. The man with the black beard and grave expression had warned her that guards had been posted on each river bank, adjacent to the islet. They had been stationed there to stop attempts such as hers. And so she had started her swim further east and was using the outpouring of the river to ease her journey.

She smelt the sour, rancid smell of the water, tainted by the effluent of the big city. Here the river waters diluted the filth, transforming the smell of raw sewage into the dull reek of the universal city river, the smell that fish and all animals, save rats, hate, but which is tolerated by human beings, such as her, who have been brought up as river rats, scratching a living along its banks.

Now she could make out the soldiers – the guards left behind on the island after the spectacle to protect the place from relic hunters. They were sitting huddled round a small fire for warmth, playing dice, talking and dozing. And she imagined (although she could not from her distance see) the hourglass in their midst, turned and turned again during the course of that long night. At each turning, one of the guards would rise and leave his companions around the fire to perform a lonely circuit of the island, making sure all was well.

This is how the bearded man had told her it would be. She understood the need for the utmost care. Lives could easily be mislaid on nights like this, particularly unimportant lives such as hers, gutter lives that survived by cunning and daring, the sort of lives big cities bred unintentionally – and, unintentionally, allowed to die, sooner rather than later.

This was a dream like no other. Jennie was its chief actor, a participant in a medieval tragedy that seemed to concern her, yet – logically – could not concern her. What was more, she was participating not as herself, but in some other form, yet one that fitted her like a glove. She it was, who had been approached by the man with the black beard and the grave expression and instructed what she must do. In return he had promised she would be paid in silver. 'More silver than thou hast ever seen in thy sweet life,' he had said. But he was well aware that the sum required would be paltry. Such as she, in her short and threadbare life, had only clutched a few sous to her breast at any one time.

Waiting, practically submerged at the water's edge, for the guard to pass on his circuit, the cold struck sharply into her frail body. When the guard had strode by, she stole out of the water and crept, belly close to the ground like a frightened mongrel (which was what she was), up the slope of the land to the execution site. 'There will be the remains of two fires,' the bearded man had told her. 'With thy back towards Notre Dame, thou must go for the right-hand pile of ashes. This is important. Thou must remember. The right-hand pile of ashes. If thou cheatest me and go for the other pile, I shall know and I shall kill thee.'

She realised it was an idle threat. He could never know which pile of ashes she searched, but one pile was as good as another to her and she had no thought of cheating. Why should she?

Crouching damply by the remains of the execution fires, still almost flat against the ground so as not to break the skyline and be seen by the guards around their fire at the water's edge, she raked through the still-warm ashes with her fingers. She took pleasure from the warmth, but in the darkness found it difficult to distinguish between charred wood and charred bone. Touch and instinct were her only guides. Before long she had collected a little pile of what she believed was bone. She must not delay. It would soon be tine for the next circuit of the guards. She stuffed the tiny fragments into a pocket of her ragged and sodden smock, the only clothing that concealed her nakedness, but the best bone – a small finger bone, but unbroken and perfect in every way, she popped into her mouth so as not to run the risk of losing it during her swim.

Halfway back across the river, drifting downstream in the current to clear the guarded portion of the banks, she became aware of an uncomfortable tingling in her mouth. At first the bone had seemed unpleasantly warm, but that sensation soon faded and for a time her mouth was comfortable. Then the tingling began – faintly at first, but growing more intense every second. Soon discomfort became pain, and pain became agony; but still she swam on, her eyes blinded by her tears. At last, on the river bank, she spat out the bone, feeling her whole mouth had become one gaping, bleeding sore. And there was a smell of burning, deep inside her head, and flashing lights like leaping flames and a suffocating heat that made her cough and retch by turn.

Suddenly there was a blinding flash and her body fell away. The blow on the back of her head, that had felled her, released her from her body, and as she floated away, she mused that the form, she had so recently occupied, did not look a bit like her. What was more, it was not the body of a girl that lay on the river bank, surrounded by a ring of evil men. It was that of a young boy of about twelve or thirteen years of age.

As Jennie struggled towards consciousness, the leaping flames became brighter and the suffocating heat thick with smoke. In her ears was a deafening roar, as of a mighty furnace – and, as realisation dawned, the furnace became her bedroom in Bangalore, but her bedroom, transported into Hieronymus Bosch's vision of hell.

Chapter Seventeen

The Reverend La Cour, rector of St Saviour's, picked up his copy of the *Guernsey Press* and read with horror the story of the destruction by fire of a bungalow on the outskirts of St Peter Port – a bungalow named Bangalore.

'The poor, poor lady,' he murmured. He had thought many times about Jennie since their conversation. He did not know her name, but he did remember Bangalore, the name of her house. This she had mentioned during their chat and it had stuck in his mind because, when he was a young parson and burning with evangelical zeal, he had almost taken up an appointment in an Anglican mission in Bangalore. 'The poor, poor lady,' he repeated.

He had been disappointed, when Jennie had not come to the organ recital, but he had hardly expected she would. It was a long way to drive for a cup of coffee and a couple of Mrs La Page's rock buns. There was the chance of a little human contact, of course – and that he felt she was badly lacking. 'However great her need; too far to come. So sad.' And he murmured again, 'The poor, poor lady.'

His wife regarded him from the other side of the breakfast table. 'What are you muttering about, Leonard?' she asked.

He thrust the newspaper across the table to her. 'You remember me telling you, my dear, about the lady who wanted to talk about her house – and about her fear of what she thought was an evil influence in a basement she had just discovered. Well, look there. That I believe must be she – Mrs Jennie James. I never knew her name before; but the property was definitely called Bangalore.'

The Reverend La Cour's wife could see the signs of 'a Christian act' coming on; but she made no comment. Most of the day the Reverend La Cour thought about 'the Bangalore mystery', as the local newspaper called it, and eventually made up his mind what he had to do. He told his wife of his decision. 'If it is she (my lady with the basement) I must go to her. She's injured and in Princess Elizabeth Hospital, they say in the paper. She is a stranger on the island and I'm sure she is rather lonely. What she needs now is a friendly face.'

'If that's what you believe, Leonard, of course you must go,' replied his wife, withstanding the temptation to tut her tongue and make hurtful remarks about 'lame ducks'. Leonard could never understand how some people resented strange parsons bumbling into their affairs at inopportune moments. She hoped this was not to be another of those times, when his good-natured attempts to help would be construed as interference. The slights he often received on these occasions were deeply wounding to him – to his wife, too, who knew he was only trying to do 'a Christian act'.

Right at the end of the afternoon visiting session at the Princess Elizabeth Hospital, Jennie opened her eyes and looked up into the kindly face of the Reverend La Cour. She had become used to spending visiting hours alone and so this unexpected visitor took her by surprise. He smiled, took her hand as it lay on the bedclothes and held it for an instant between his own.

'Ah, it is you,' he said. 'I thought it must be from the newspaper report. How are you, Mrs James?'

Jennie smiled wanly. 'Yes, it's me all right,' she replied. 'I am surprised to see you. It's very nice of you to come.'

'I'm afraid I'm a little late, and the sister won't let me stay long – she says it's important that I don't tire you – but she did allow me to have a brief word.' He smiled down at her, a great, grey, comfortably lined moon of a face, swimming above her bed. 'Did I give you the wrong advice, Mrs James, the other day when we met? I do hope I did not.'

'No, not the wrong advice. I think you gave me the best advice anyone could possibly have given. I went on and found out what I needed to know; and you were right; it is better to know than to guess. At least my horrors have substance now, and in a way it makes them more easy to bear.'

He took her hand again and patted it, like you would a friendly puppy, thought Jennie. 'And it seems you, too, were right, my dear – about the evil influence. At the time I found it difficult to believe; but now it would appear your presentiments were well founded. The human mind is a wonderful device, I always say. What a dreadful thing to have happened, though.'

Jennie's pale face looked back at him; but there was no longer the tense, hunted look he had seen in her eyes the last time they met. Now, in its stead, there was a new confidence and an unexpected strength. 'I don't want to talk about Bangalore, if it's all the same to you. It's too painful and anyway I mustn't get anyone else involved. It's all over now; and it's as though a great weight has been lifted from my mind. Now I just need to forget.'

'Of course, I understand completely.' The Reverend La Cour smiled comfortingly down at her. Should he offer another little prayer? No, he thought not. 'Now you must rest, my dear. Before I leave, though, I wanted you to know that if there is anything I can do to help, you only have to ask. You know where I am and I should be very pleased to do whatever I can. Do you have somewhere to go, when you're better?'

'Yes, thank you. A friend on Alderney will help me with everything, I think; but it's very kind of you to offer.'

'God bless you, my dear. I hope to see you sometime at St Saviour's, when you're well.' He took out a notebook and scribbled something on a page and tore it out. 'My telephone number. Remember; anything I can do. Anything at all. Give me a ring.' He laid the sheet of paper on Jennie's bedside locker.

The old man turned and walked slowly away along the ward. That evening he found he could not get Jennie out of his mind. He was puzzled by the change that had come over her, the new strength he had detected in her eyes. 'And after such a shock, too,' he murmured. 'People are very surprising.'

His wife looked up from her needlework. 'You're muttering again, Leonard,' she gently scolded.

'Yes, my dear; I suppose I am,' he replied. All that evening questions flew around in his head. What had Mrs James found out about Bangalore? And had her discovery unleashed the evil that she had sensed so strongly? Could this evil have been responsible for the fire; and most importantly, was the evil now spent, or merely dormant, lying in wait?

The Reverend La Cour's thoughts returned again and again to the change in Jennie. He had seen similar changes in other people, but under different circumstances – the precise nature of these, he could not recall. Then, suddenly, it came to him. In Jennie's face was the kind of strength he had sometimes noted in those who knew, and accepted, that they only had a limited time to live.

*

For three weeks the mystery of the Bangalore telephone number vaguely flitted in and out of John Frensham's mind. He had never been noted as an impulsive man of action, and his pursuit of a solution to the breakdown of telephone links with his friend on Guernsey was treated with characteristic sloth. It wasn't that he lacked interest in Jennie and her affairs; it was just that he believed that most questions had a habit of answering themselves, if left alone long enough. The waywardness of Jennie's telephone number would have a logical explanation – of that he was sure; it was just a matter of letting time unravel the mystery.

When it had not done so in three weeks, however, and no explanatory note had appeared in the post from Jennie, John decided that the time had come for action. He packed a small suitcase, took a train to Southampton and boarded the overnight ferry to the Channel Islands. Arriving at St Peter Port after a cold and distinctly uncomfortable crossing, John made himself at home in the back seat of a taxi and demanded to be taken to Bangalore. 'It's a house on the St Martin's road,' he told the driver in response to the latter's incredulous stare.

The driver looked strangely at him through the rearview mirror. 'If that's what you really want,' he said. 'But you know what happened to it, I suppose. There ain't much of it left.'

'Not much of it left. What on earth do you mean?' John, after a night at sea on an inhospitable Channel, was in no mood for playing guessing games with a Guernsey taxi driver.

'They say it was lightning,' the driver told him with a non-committal Gallic shrug, 'but no one knows. It was a filthy night, that's for sure. Set itself on fire, Bangalore did – right in the middle of the night – and burnt to the ground before the fire brigade could get there. It was busy at the time pumping out the basement of Government House Hotel – the fire brigade was, I mean. That's the sort of night it was.'

'How long ago was this?' asked John.

'About a month, I reckon,' replied the driver, and then, in a slightly belligerent tone, 'Well, do you want to go, or not?' One of his most profitable hours of the day – when the mainland ferry docked – was ticking away, and still he didn't know if he had a fare or not.

'Yes, yes, take me there – take me there first, anyway.' John thought for a while and then, as they drove away from the harbour, asked, 'Was anyone hurt?'

'Not badly hurt, as you might say. The lady, what lived there, broke her leg escaping from the flames and they say she was badly shocked. But I reckon she'd feel herself lucky to get away with that, in the circumstances, like. It was a truly evil blaze by all accounts. The house was completely destroyed. Lucky there was no one killed, if you ask me. If there'd been more than the one floor, I doubt the lady would've escaped. That was the sort of fire it were. Whoosh... all gone in a minute or two.'

At Bangalore the destruction was indeed complete. The whole of the roof had disappeared; as well as the verandahs and all the windows and doors throughout the bungalow. Even some of the external walls had collapsed, leaving others more or less intact. The great granite fireplace stood alone and battle-scarred. John walked for a time amongst the ruins, whilst the taxi waited. Already the verdant Guernsey undergrowth was beginning to infiltrate into the blackened area of the site around the ruined house. But of Jennie's home, nothing was left; her beautifully fitted kitchen, her furniture, all her personal effects, everything had been reduced to piles of charred rubbish. In what had once been the garage at the end of the wing furthest from the kitchen, stood the blackened and twisted remains of Jennie's Morris Minor.

To think that a complete home can be reduced to this. There's absolutely nothing left, thought John. He had seen many incinerated homes during the war, usually the result of German incendiary bombs, but destruction such as this, was totally beyond his experience. Its thoroughness had no equal. 'Poor, poor Jennie,' he muttered. 'What will she do now?'

He returned to the taxi. The driver was now as happy as a sandboy. With his meter ticking away, he was prepared to comply unquestioningly with the least of John's requests; whether they involved driving, waiting or talking, it was all the same to him. He was being paid; and, out of season, having a tame mainlander on board was one of the most prized acquisitions of a Guernsey taxi driver. Judicious suggestions as to possible destinations invariably could enlarge the ultimate charge – as well as the hoped-for tip. Such rich pickings rarely were available when an islander occupied the back seat.

'I don't suppose you know what happened to Mrs James, the lady who used to live here? Any idea where she might be?'

To inhabitants of a big city, or to less inquisitive parts of the British Isles, such a question would have seemed pointless, but John had learnt this much from his stay with Jennie: on Guernsey, everyone's business was a matter of public concern.

'Can't help you there, I'm afraid,' replied the driver, 'but if you want, we could pop down to the police station. I'm sure they'd be able to tell you.'

At the police station, a sergeant was suitably sympathetic to John's request for information. He read from the report of the incident, which took place in the early morning hours of 18th March. 'Let's see that would be three weeks ago, sir, almost to the day,' explained the sergeant. 'The owner – Mrs James – was alone in the house at the time of the fire and she made her escape via the bedroom window. In so doing, she fell and broke her leg. She managed to drag herself clear of the building, though, and when our patrol car arrived on the scene, she was lying on the lawn, sir, in a fairly poor way, I would say. The ambulance arrived about ten minutes later and she was taken to the Princess Elizabeth Hospital. What happened to her after that, I don't know.'

'What started the fire?' asked John.

The police sergeant shrugged his shoulders. 'Really couldn't say for certain. It was a rough old night, bucketing down with rain, but not a real thunderstorm, if you see what I mean. It could have been a freak lightning strike, or an electrical fault. We have no reason to suspect any foul play and the insurance company inspector has made a thorough examination and, whilst he did seem puzzled, he hasn't raised any objections to the settlement of the claim.'

'And Mrs James now? You can give me no idea where I might be able to find her?'

'Afraid not, sir,' replied the sergeant. 'I'm sure she'll have left the hospital by now, but the Almoner's Office there might be able to tell you where she is convalescing.'

Thanking the sergeant, John left the station and instructed the taxi driver to take him to the Princess Elizabeth Hospital. Here the Almoner's Office proved extremely helpful. The lady there explained that Mrs James had been treated for shock, a broken leg and minor cuts and abrasions, these latter injuries presumably caused by a fall she had sustained as she was escaping from the blazing building and pulling herself clear of the fire. Whilst in hospital, she had received visits from a friend from Alderney and it was to Alderney that she had gone on her discharge, one week after her admission. Any after-care, John was told, would be given by the hospital on that island.

John asked if the almoner had any record of an address and telephone number of Mrs James's present residence. After consulting her superior, the lady agreed to give these to John, bearing in mind that he was an old friend of Mrs James and was only on the island for a flying visit.

By the time he left the Princess Elizabeth Hospital, most of the morning had slipped away and the taxi driver was feeling extremely satisfied with the sizeable sum that was recorded on his meter. This sort of hire was an unlikely windfall at this time of year.

'Right,' said John, sinking into the well-used, lumpy back seat of the taxi, 'the Old Government House Hotel in town please.'

The taxi paid off, a room booked for one night, a quick wash and brush up, and John was seated in the dining room of the hotel anticipating an enjoyable meal. The question was, what to do now? Clearly Jennie had no need of him, now she had this author in tow. Possibly a good thing, too; more suited to her impulsive character, maybe, than boring, dependable John Frensham. Sadly he examined the address that had been written down for him by the lady almoner: *Mrs Jennie James, c/o Clive Dumas, Fort Colombé, Alderney.* John Frensham had no illusions. There was no place for him in this scenario.

That afternoon he wrote a short letter to Jennie, expressing concern over the disaster that had taken place, and enquiring tactfully about her future plans. Next day he departed on the ferry for the mainland and his safe and dependable little home in Guildford.

Chapter Eighteen

'It was just a coincidence, Jennie. Nothing more than a silly coincidence. They happen all the time. Nothing to concern yourself about. It had no sinister significance, of that I'm sure.'

Since she had come to Fort Colombé, it had become Clive Dumas's daily chore to try to convince her that there was no evil connection between the date of the fire at Bangalore and the fourteenth-century happenings on an island in the River Seine at Paris. Maybe in his innermost heart, he did not believe his own words, but he had no doubt that it was important that Jennie should believe them. This would be the last occasion they would have this argument. Afterwards, by mutual consent, they would file away their thoughts on the subject and speak of it no more. But today; one last effort at understanding was being made.

They were walking along the cliff-top path near Fort Colombé. More accurately, Clive was walking and Jennie was hobbling, still struggling to get back the normal use of her once-broken leg. Dumas was delighted to see how much progress she had made. Her stick, so recently a very necessary aid to walking, was now used much more frequently as a scythe, as she waged war on fronds of bracken that were forever encroaching on to the pathway.

Jennie was becoming peeved. Why was Clive being so obtuse? Taking a particularly vicious swipe at a nettle, she said, 'How could it be a coincidence? Some coincidence, when there are 364 other days in the year to choose from. Come on, Clive; think about it: twelve months with a number eighteen in them, so there are eleven other eighteens to go for. Why choose the one in March? How could it be just coincidence that my fire happens on the same day of the same month when de Molay, the Grand Master of the Knights Templar was burned at the stake? Don't you realise, Bangalore might have been blazing away at the very hour King Philippe's thugs pushed their fire brands into the pyres that were to burn the living bodies of de Molay and de Charney? It's just too gruesome; and too much of a coincidence.'

Clive Dumas noted with a gentle tolerance her animated defence of her belief – certainty, even – of the significance of the date of the fire. He tried to allow the subject to drop. There seemed no point in persisting. He looked at Jennie with a deep affection. Now the horror was passed, he was overjoyed to see she was developing into a different person, more relaxed, more cheerful and with a quiet inner radiance that he found so beguiling. This was the old Jennie of years long gone, a Jennie he had never known, one that had been stifled by the death of Greg. Maybe, but for the influence of Bangalore, the old Jennie would have reemerged earlier; but now, at last, the period of waiting was over and the transformation had begun.

Jennie continued, 'If only I had realised what date it was – that it was the eve of de Molay's burning – when I drove you back to the airport – I would never have returned to Bangalore – not after what you had just told me. I would have been mad to do such a thing. As it was, I'd no idea of the date.' She took another swipe at a nettle, turned and smiled at Dumas. 'I should have gone straight to an hotel and stayed there until it was all over.'

Dumas returned her smile, nodded and said nothing. She seemed unaware that there was an alternative scenario, one that was dominant in his mind. In this, Jennie's presence at Bangalore was an essential ingredient in the disaster. If she had not returned home that night, nothing would have happened. There would have been no fire, no release of evil. The violence would still be lying there, coiled like a tightly wound spring, ready to unleash its venom, when its intended victim was present. For, according to this version of events, the malevolence at Bangalore had been directed towards Jennie, not towards the house. Hopefully now, with the house destroyed and Jennie far away from its influence, the ghost had been laid – and Jennie could begin to live again. Maybe her night of terror – a night about which she would not speak in detail – had been a necessary stage in the exorcism.

None of this, however, did Clive impart to Jennie. Nor did he admit to her that, if he, too, had realised, on that fateful day, what the date was, he would never have returned to Alderney, leaving her, alone and unprotected, to face whatever lay in wait for her at Bangalore. No meeting with the States of Alderney was more important than Jennie's safety. If only he had thought! His only excuse was that the surfeit of fact and speculation that he had absorbed in the preceding twenty-four hours, must have dulled his reasoning powers.

*

But that was all in the past now. The day after his return to Alderney, Dumas had tried to ring Jennie and getting the unobtainable tone, had consulted his contacts on the island. They had told him of the fire, which was then the most lively piece of island gossip. Within hours, he was at Jennie's bedside, almost before she had realised what had happened to her. Since then, they had become practically inseparable, completely enveloped in each other's lives.

On her release from hospital, Jennie had come to Colombé, practically immobilised by a huge plaster cast (she had christened her 'armour') on her left leg, her face drawn and weary and still bearing the scars of her struggle to escape the flames of her burning home. Her sleep, too, was still racked by nightmares. Now, however, things had improved. The plaster cast had been removed, all traces of the scars had disappeared and she had stopped screaming in her sleep.

The complete change of scene had worked miracles on her appearance. The worry lines, that had visibly increased during the last weeks at Bangalore, were gradually fading. She walked every morning on the cliff top, watching the spring flowers fade and be replaced by the flowers of early summer, hearing the sea birds cry and watching the ever-changing seascape stretched out below her and away towards the coast of France.

Here, high on the cliff, she had discovered a favourite place. Most days, when the weather was fine, she came there, usually alone, leaving Clive at work at his desk in the big room of the fort. In this fold on the cliff top she could feel completely at peace, enjoying its isolation and freedom. Here, maybe, she allowed herself to dwell on those private thoughts she never gave voice to; for she, just as Clive, had secrets – about what, we shall never know – perhaps about the night of the fire, or of her presentiments of the future. All we know for certain is that these thoughts were stowed away in a secluded recess of her mind, skilfully hidden from everyone's view by her cheerful, everyday disposition and only taken out, dusted and mulled over in the strictest privacy.

At other times Jennie was wholly absorbed by an all-consuming joy of the present. She dreamed of travel, of the hot perfumed scent of the Provençal countryside, of exploring the ancient villages of south-west France, of wine, of sunshine and the buzz of a million bees at work amongst the peach blossom. She dreamed of all these things, which she wished to experience and share with Clive. But not now – not quite yet.

In fact for many weeks neither she nor Clive mentioned the future. There seemed to be an unspoken agreement between them. Together they enjoyed total absorption in a private world that only had a present – no past, no future, just a day-to-day here-and-now. In this Elysian existence, it is hardly surprising that love – maybe alive before, but unacknowledged – should begin to flourish.

At first it was a tentative, almost a fearful thing, the physical aspect of love being complicated by Jennie's 'armour' and her healing wounds. But as time passed and Jennie was restored to fitness, their relationship broke through the externally imposed barriers and took on a life of its own.

Clive was astonished by the effect his changed circumstances had on his work. Previously he had found love affairs disturbing, imposing demands that he had found irksome and ruinous to his concentration. Such sad experiences had convinced him that permanent love was not for him and that he was condemned to a solitary life. Now, however, the experience was entirely different. His relationship with Jennie caused no disruption. Instead it seemed to bring a deeper understanding to his work, providing an all-enveloping calm within which stress disappeared and imagination could blossom.

In time an understanding grew between Jennie and Clive – an understanding that convalescence was over and a life of cohabitation had begun; but how, when and why this occurred, they did not know or care.

⋆

Only one incident from the outside world, one that happened at the very outset of Jennie's time at Colombé, disturbed their mutual absorption. It was the letter John Frensham had posted in St Peter Port. This had come as a surprise to Jennie. It had never occurred to her that she ought to have told John of her escape from the Bangalore blaze. It was only when she read his seemingly aggrieved letter that she felt a spasm of guilt. Of course she should have thought of John; but truth to tell, after the fire, she had thought of no one but herself and Clive. John's interest in her life had been completely forgotten. 'Oh, how cruel of me,' cried Jennie. 'After all his kindness to me. How could I?'

But now, when she thought of John's dash across the Channel to her aid, like some medieval knight to the assistance of a damsel in distress, she felt desolate. The only person for whom she had hankered, after the fire, had been Clive.

★

Having become lovers, the idea of even temporary separation was unthinkable for Jennie and Clive. Together they paid a flying visit to London to replace some, at least, of Jennie's lost wardrobe and personal effects.

'It really is quite surprising how little you actually need to get by,' Jennie had said as they dashed around Marks and Spencer's in Oxford Street. 'You can manage with very little, when you have to.'

'It's nice not to have to,' laughed Clive.

Their trip developed into a round of self-indulgence. 'Spending the ill-gotten gains,' Jennie called it, referring to her insurance pay-out, which she considered as belonging almost as much to Clive as to herself. They visited theatres, fitted in a ballet at Covent Garden, saw the latest films and indulged in lavish meals in expensive restaurants.

It was at this time they contemplated a visit to John Frensham in Guildford and decided, rather grudgingly, that it was the thing to do. However, when Jennie tried several times to telephone him, and was greeted by his answering machine, she replaced the receiver with a guilty feeling of relief. The prospect of the two of them having to confront John's disappointed (even disapproving) expression, was not relished by Jennie. At last, after a number of abortive calls, it became clear that John was away from home. Jennie cheerfully left a message on the machine and she and Clive got on with the business of enjoying themselves.

Returning to Fort Colombé was, for Jennie, like coming home. She was amazed how quickly she had settled into her new surroundings with her new partner. After all the worry of the past months, she was now deliriously happy. 'How can I ever repay you for all your kindness and help, dear, dearest Clive?' she exclaimed one day.

'You could marry me,' suggested Clive.

'Yes, oh yes please,' replied Jennie, throwing her arms about his neck. 'But not now; not just yet. It might spoil things.'

Clive kissed her nose and said, 'How could it spoil anything?' But he did not pursue the subject. A date in October loomed in his mind. After that date was over, maybe. Until then, enjoy what there was to enjoy and be ever vigilant; that was Clive's unspoken strategy. He wondered if the significance of 13th October had occurred to Jennie as well – particularly as in this year, 13th October would fall on a Friday.

Chapter Nineteen

John Frensham had been visiting his sister in Manchester, when Jennie and Clive had made their trip to London. On his return home, he listened to the messages on his answering machine. They were few in number – and those, that there were, were pretty mundane: the secretary of the bowls club, wanting to arrange a meeting; the vicar with a query about the parochial church council minutes; Mrs Smythe-Jones offering an invitation to one of her dinner parties – luckily long since passed by the time John listened to the tape. (He could not stand Mrs Smythe-Jones, nor her dinner parties.) And then there was Jennie, an over-excited Jennie, John decided, clearly enjoying herself with her new man.

However hard he tried, John could not help having mean, unpleasant thoughts about Clive Dumas. It should have been he, John Frensham, who had successfully rushed to Jennie's aid after that dreadful fire, not some long-haired arty chap living in a fort on Alderney. It was at times like this that John realised that the wounds of Jennie's persistent refusal to marry him were still unhealed. Yet he never allowed himself to admit for one instant a very relevant fact: that he was, in his own way, still in love with her. Had the idea been suggested to him, he would have denied it with considerable force. For did he not always have his emotions well under control?

After his abortive humanitarian dash to Guernsey, he had received a contrite letter from Jennie, apologising for not letting him know about the fire and thanking him for his concern which, she said, she did not deserve. But it wasn't contrition, John wanted from Jennie; it was Jennie herself – herself as she had been in the days before her Guernsey adventure, the Jennie he had admired and loved from afar, the Jennie that Greg had had the good fortune to win – and, according to John, had never truly appreciated.

John Frensham had re-read Jennie's last letter many times, trying to make sense of the hints it contained of something vaguely sinister to do with the disastrous fire.

> *...What I hadn't realised was that the date when it happened was a very special one, as far as Bangalore was concerned. It's a long and involved story and one that I'm sure you would just pooh-pooh, if I told you – as you have pooh-poohed all my other ramblings-on about the Bangalore basement. Anyway, by the time the fire happened, there was simply no doubt in my mind that the basement had been used for some quite hideous activities, and these had left their mark on the place. What's more, the roots of these goings-on stretched way back in time, into the Middle Ages even. The German connection was really a quite modern addition.*
>
> *I don't suppose this makes any sense to you at all, but there we are. Best just accept what I say, and don't get involved. I got involved and look what happened to me! Anyway, I shall never look for a dream house again. I found one once, and it turned into a nightmare. What I shall do now, I haven't even begun to think, but one thing is certain, I won't be coming back to the mainland.*

'Not coming back to the mainland,' John had mused, 'after all that's happened! I'm sure she's mad – or in love,' he added glumly.

Having missed the opportunity of meeting her during her visit to the mainland, he realised just how mixed were his feelings; at once disappointed and relieved. 'Is this the end?' he wondered. 'I suppose it must be.' What else could it be?

*

On Alderney, summer faded imperceptibly into autumn – the sort of long, warm golden autumn, which the Channel Islands often have the good luck to enjoy. Clive and Jennie lay on the cliff top beside the fort, basking in the late sunshine and their own idyllic happiness. They were contented to be on their own, safe in each other's company. Even their short trips over the bumpy roads to St Anne's were rare – disturbing disruptions to the even tenor of their days and, therefore, put off again and again until they became essential.

During September a letter arrived for Clive from Le Messurier. It popped up out of the blue, at a time when Clive wanted to forget all about the Knights Templar and Bangalore. He read it without relish, and as he did, he could hear the man's peevish little voice uttering the words that were to ruin his peace of mind.

You certainly stirred up a hornets' nest with your enquiries about the Templars a few months ago, didn't you? All the people in the know have been buzzing with the news ever since, particularly after the destruction of Bangalore. Incidentally, now I realise who the mysterious lady was that you had in tow that day when you came to see me.

I understand from Fred Guilbert that you now have the more or less full story of the Templars and their connection with the island. You may, however, lack one bit of information that could have relevance to what seems to me to be a very dangerous situation – for the lady, if for no one else. Hence this letter.

I gather Fred told you about the trade in relics that went on after de Molay's execution and the curse which is said to attach to genuine relics; well there is strong evidence that one of the genuine relics came to Guernsey with the escaping fleet. There is no tangible proof of its existence after the fleet's arrival, but the presence of some, apparently authentic, relic was fundamental to the Templar society on Guernsey – the one that was infiltrated by the Germans before the war. This relic is probably still in existence somewhere at Bangalore. The burning down of the property, if you believe in all this mumbo-jumbo, certainly seems to suggest that it is. Clearly Mrs Grace didn't know about it, or if she did, never dealt with it properly. Your lady friend became the unintentional keeper of the relic, when she bought the property. Later, after she started asking too many public questions, she made herself vulnerable to the curse.

I write to tell you this, not in any mood of malice, but as a friendly warning that the curse has not yet been fulfilled. The burning of the house was just a warning. Best of luck. This will certainly teach you in the future to avoid meddling in affairs, of which you have no knowledge.

There was a postscript too. It read:

PS Oh by the way. The proper method of dealing with the relic, if you find it, is to bury it with due respect. This way you might avoid becoming the next unintentional custodian. Sleep well.

'"Bury it with due respect"? Whatever that means,' muttered Clive Dumas to himself, laying aside the letter with a feeling of apprehension. Dumas, the natural optimist, suddenly tasted the unfamiliar bitterness of expected and imminent disaster. He knew he could not tell Jennie about the contents of the letter. This was another secret he had to carry alone. What was more vital, if Le Messurier was right, something had to be done about the relic, and done quickly. The time was running out. He looked at the calendar. It was already 7th September. There was no time to lose.

Inventing some excuse, he made a trip to Guernsey the next day. It was the first of several day-long excursions he made, during which he combed through the ruins of Bangalore, looking for something which, if he were lucky enough to find it, he hoped (maybe vainly) he would recognise for what it was – the authentic relic of Grand Master de Molay. Every time he walked up the drive to the ruins of the bungalow, his sense of desperation increased. What hope was there of finding a piece of charred bone amid this chaos? It was like looking for the proverbial needle in a haystack – a totally impossible task; but one that he was obligated to attempt. In addition, he was depressed by having to hide the true purpose of his visits to Guernsey from Jennie, but he felt he could not disturb her apparent tranquillity with this new anxiety.

With the arrival of October, Clive's pessimism deepened. Day after day he made the trip to Bangalore; day after day he sifted through piles of debris in a slow and painstaking search that seemed never-ending. At the same time his vigilance for Jennie's safety and his attempts to surround her with an invisible web of love became more intense. If Jennie noticed a change in him, she never remarked upon it. Equally, on the surface at least, she gave no sign of any apprehension as Friday 13th October approached. Maybe she did not realise the time slipping by; or did not allow herself to think of the significance of the approaching date. Certainly she appeared happy, ridiculously happy, savouring her delight in each minute as it, butterfly-like, flitted by.

The present had become everything to her; the future appeared not to exist.

The anniversary remained undiscussed, and the silence, although founded on the most worthy of motives, that of mutual consideration, reduced the support they could give each other. Both had unknowingly created a slough of secrecy about themselves which condemned each to wallow alone and friendless. Possibly neither was sure whether the other had appreciated the significance of the approaching date. Logic, however, argued otherwise. But whilst uncertainty existed, why trigger fear? In this stalemate, who was protecting whom? Because of Jennie's last Bangalore dream, the dream from which she awoke to find her house burning around her, the dream she had never related to Clive, she was totally aware of the existence of a relic, somewhere lost within the ruins of Bangalore and she was now waiting with extraordinary control, expecting the next act in this bizarre drama to take place. Hoping against hope that, by some miracle, it would not happen; but if it did, was it not to be expected that it would happen on the anniversary of King Philippe's dawn raid upon the Templars?

Under this threat, both Jennie and Clive resorted to a simple defence – simple and as old as the hills – they adopted a siege mentality. The fort had become their sanctuary, within which they hoped that Jennie would be safe.

As the day approached, they became increasingly reclusive. They were invited to go on a fishing trip in the boat of one of Clive's friends. They both politely declined the invitation, making elaborate and apparently facetious jokes about their fear of Friday 13th. Shopping trips were postponed. Even one of Jennie's check-ups at the Alderney hospital was put off until the end of the month. The stage was set and our two actors, still not admitting their concern to each other, waited for the curtain to go up.

And this is the way they would have met the threat, besieged together in the fort, except for one factor – Clive's obsession with finding the relic. He worried over whether he could make one last trip to Bangalore. Could he leave Jennie one more time before the 13th? He had an irrational belief that success could be almost within his grasp. Having already scoured the area of the bungalow and the adjacent garden, turning over huge piles of debris by hand, only one place remained unsearched, the place most likely to contain the relic, but the one that had been the least accessible – the basement.

Painfully Clive had spent the last two visits to the ruins clearing the debris from the head of the stair and now he felt confident that he could search the basement in one last visit. Explaining to Jennie that he would have to go to Guernsey on 12th October, he watched her face for some reaction, but saw none. Her expression gave nothing away.

'If you must,' she said. 'But do be careful.' Could he detect in those words an undercurrent of concern? She drove him to the airport, kissed him goodbye and said, 'God bless. I'll pick you up tonight. I need you very much.'

And he replied, 'I need you too.'

With such platitudes, relationships, such as theirs, have been known to end.

*

Work at Bangalore started quite normally. Clive changed into the overalls that he had bought specially for his work among the ruins of Bangalore and kept hidden there in the burned out wreck of Jennie's Morris Minor. He had instructed the taxi driver to come back for him in plenty of time to catch his return flight. That left him six hours to complete his search. It was a mild, still day with light cloud occasionally masking the sun. All was prepared for the descent into the basement. Having cleared the smaller rubbish from the stair head, Clive could now crawl under a pile of larger objects, mainly composed of an unburnt section of the roof structure, and reach the stair. This, being made of cast iron, had been unharmed by the fire. Equally the strong concrete ground floor slab was undamaged. Wedging his powerful torch into a cavity in the debris, Clive began clearing the stair treads of minor rubbish.

Soon he was standing in the basement and, with the aid of his torch, began his minute search of the walls and floor. The basement being relatively free from debris, his task was fairly simple. What he was looking for was some form of niche or recess in the wall or floor (a feature overlooked during his previous examination of the basement) which might be the hiding place for the relic.

The morning passed, and still he had only completed his work in the main room. He became uncomfortably aware of the inexorable leaking away of time. Beads of sweat stood out on his forehead. He tried to work more quickly, but it was uncomfortably hot and humid in the basement and his breath began to come in painful gasps. He had been so sure – so convinced the relic would be here. He had forced himself to believe in his success, otherwise he would never have dared to leave Jennie on the eve of what he knew was probably to be the most fateful day of her life – and, maybe, of his, too.

His work in the guard room did not take long. Once more he found nothing. Clive staggered back to the stairs and collapsed on the bottom tread, the first time that day that he had allowed himself a pause in his work. It was two o'clock. Only two hours left before the return of the taxi – but just one room remaining, the small room near the foot of the stair. Panic seized him. The relic must be there; *it had to be*. No longer did he question its existence. If there were no relic, he argued, there could be no logical explanation for all the strange happenings at Bangalore – Jennie's dreams, the existence of the basement, the conspiracy of silence among the locals, the fire. Yet could logic be applied when the whole rigmarole defied reason? Whether or not, panic had at last driven Clive Dumas through his barrier of disbelief; he now accepted unquestioningly, irrationally, the whole weird tale of the Templars, the relic and the curse. He was convinced – and being convinced, he knew there was only one thing he could do: find the relic and give it a burial 'with respect'. If he failed, Jennie was in the most appalling danger.

Leaping from the stairs, he prized open the door into the small room and was met by an invisible blanket of stale air, still tainted with the smell of burning. Choking and gasping, Clive forced himself to enter the small, claustrophobic space, muttering to himself, 'It must be here. It's got to be here.'

Minute by minute time was seeping away. He found himself obsessively counting the seconds as he commenced the final part of his search. The walls yielded nothing. The floor, however, was partially covered by a thin layer of trampled-down dirt. It was like sawdust, maybe once spread to absorb a spillage of liquid, now dry and dark grey in colour. Clive scraped furiously at this layer with a piece of wood, pushing the dirt into heaps so that he could see the surface of the floor beneath; searching, always searching, for an irregularity that might indicate a trap door. At last his efforts were rewarded. In the centre of the floor was a square, surrounded by a joint – a concrete slab containing a lifting insert.

After repeated and unsuccessful attempts to lift the slab, Clive climbed the stair and, finding a length of steel bar in the pile of debris, arched over the stairwell, prized it free.

Using this as a lever, angled over a block of wood, he at last managed to raise the slab. As he did so, there was a tremendous crash from above, and the collapsed roof structure, under which he had crawled to reach the stair, fell, blocking his escape. Clive's clumsy withdrawal of the steel bar must have destabilised the delicate balance of the debris. And now he was trapped.

The significance of what had happened did not immediately dawn on Clive. He was too interested in what the cavity in the floor contained. Laying aside the concrete slab, he looked down through a pane of glass set in a wooden-frame, into a hollow, two feet square and about two feet deep. The cavity was lined with a fine, dark blue velvet. Raising the glass cover, Clive ran his hands around the velvet surfaces. This merely served to confirm what his eyes had already told him. The space, that certainly once could have contained the relic, was empty.

★

Arriving back at the site in good time to pick up his fare, the taxi driver, Bert Guillaume, parked his car beside the gate at the end of Bangalore's drive and settled down to wait, listening to his radio. When the rendezvous time arrived and Clive Dumas had still not appeared, Bert Guillaume began to wonder if something untoward might have happened. He had carried this passenger on similar missions to Bangalore a couple of times before and on each occasion Clive had appeared at the gate meticulously on time, ready for the return trip to the airport. Bert gave him ten minutes more and then went to investigate.

By the time he was halfway along the drive, he could hear Clive's cries for help. After an hour of fruitless attempts to shift the pile of debris that blocked the top of the stairs, Clive was worn out; his hands were bleeding, his clothes were torn and he was filthy from head to foot. All the while as he struggled, he was imagining the Alderney flight, leaving without him and Jennie waiting fruitlessly for his return. To have failed in his search for the relic was bad enough, but to have failed and not to return to Fort Colombé for the beginning of Friday 13th, he believed was tantamount to a betrayal of Jennie, just at the time when she needed his support the most. He knew that if he did not catch that plane, there was no chance of crossing to Alderney that night. He could not even hire a private plane, because Alderney airport would close for the night immediately after the arrival of the Inter-Island flight from Guernsey. These were the thoughts that were tormenting him, as he tugged and pushed at the obstruction at the head of the stairs.

Bert Guillaume examined the situation with a philosophic detachment. 'You'll never shift that, mate,' he announced cheerfully. 'I'll get some help. I've got a friend with a dozer.'

Half an hour later, Clive Dumas was free – but bitterly unhappy. It was exactly the time the Alderney flight was scheduled to take off, and he was still about twenty-minutes' drive away from the airport. 'Get me to a phone quickly, will you?' he shouted to Bert.

Clive's intention was to plead with the airline authorities to delay the take-off of the Alderney plane, but the opening words of the airline representative dashed his hopes: 'The Alderney flight has just this minute taken off, sir. You would like to be booked on the early morning flight tomorrow?'

Clive agreed with a sick feeling in the pit of his stomach. There was nothing else he could do. What was more, he couldn't even ring up Jennie to warn her that he would not be on the flight. She would already be on her way to the airport to meet him. As a last resort he rang up Alderney airport and left a message there for Jennie. It was a poor substitute, but at least he could explain his absence and tell her he would be returning early the next morning.

Then, realising that everything had been done that could be done to alleviate a disastrous situation, he walked back to the taxi and asked Bert Guillaume to take him to the Airport Hotel. The drive was a silent one. Parked at the foot of the steps up to the hotel entrance, Clive said to Bert, 'Thanks for all your help. I don't know what I should have done without you.'

'No more don't I, mate,' replied the ever-cheerful Bert. 'I don't suppose you wanted to stay in that hole all night, did you? Hope missing the flight hasn't put you out too much.'

You will never know how much, thought Clive, as he handed Fred a generous tip.

Later that night, after three abortive attempts to ring Jennie, Clive asked the telephone authority to test the line and was told it was out of order. They would report the problem to the engineers in the morning, he was informed. Evidently there was to be no sleep for Clive that night.

⋆

There was little sleep, too, for Reverend La Cour, the rector of St Saviour's. In the early hours of the morning, he moved in his semi-wakefulness and moaned. Beside him, from her single bed, pushed up close to his, his wife put out a hand and touched his shoulder.

'Leonard; what's the matter? Can't you sleep?'

Now fully awake, he turned on his back and groaned. 'I'm so worried about that lady, the one who was hurt in the fire,' he said. 'You know the one I mean. Mrs James – that was her name, wasn't it? For some reason or other I can't get her out of my thoughts tonight. I fear she's in great danger.'

'Nonsense,' replied his wife. 'Much more likely you've got indigestion after eating those pickled onions at supper.' Mrs La Cour was not an imaginative lady.

'Oh my dear, I can tell the difference between indigestion of the body and an unquiet mind. I'm sure she is in the most dreadful danger. I have a presentiment of enormous evil and malicious forces. I really fear for her safety.'

He lay for a while, staring into the blackness of the bedroom, whilst the sensation of evil engulfed him. Then, with a sigh, he rose, put on his dressing gown and descended to his study. There he knelt at an ancient faldstool, his head bent in prayer – and there he maintained vigil, until the first traces of dawn appeared in the eastern sky. Then he rose and returned to his bed; but still his troubled mind would not relax in sleep.

Chapter Twenty

In the early hours of the morning on Friday, 13th October, when the sky was clear and a crescent moon was drawing a silver track across the strangely quiet sea below Colombé Point, just at the hour when King Philippe's soldiers were preparing to beat on the gates of the Templars' strongholds over six hundred years before, Charles Grace stood in her bedroom and beckoned Jennie to follow him.

No explanation was needed. His words of many months before, and the warning they contained, returned to her mind. 'In your search for the truth, be careful you do not unleash the evil that lies within and beyond us all.' She had persisted in her quest; now she was about to pay the penalty for her dedication.

She felt no fear. Only two emotions filled her mind: relief that soon all would be over, and thankfulness that Clive was not there to witness the *dénouement*. For she had made a bargain with Providence: in return for her life, Clive Dumas would be spared. It was the sort of bargain about which you can never be completely certain. You never really know whether Providence has received your message, and even less, whether it has agreed to the terms. But Jennie, despite all the tension and pain that her brief life on Guernsey had caused her, still, for some inexplicable reason, placed her trust in Charles Grace. And so when he stood beside her bed and beckoned to her, she went willingly – a dutiful sacrifice to the curse of de Molay. It was unjust – she knew that – to involve her, who had not the slightest complicity in the evil done all those years ago. Yet she had learnt not to expect justice and fairness, according to human standards, in this life, but to retain unbounded hope for justice in the next. That marked Jennie James down as special, different. For she could 'unleash the evil that lies within and beyond' and still retain her optimism.

If there had been human witnesses of the strange events of that night, they would have seen two figures – one man, one woman – dressed in white, descending the path from the Colombé headland to the horseshoe of sand below, gleaming silver in the moonlight. They, these human witnesses which did not exist, would have watched as the two white figures, insubstantial against the silver sand and only one of them casting a shadow, moved to the water's edge, and then out, out along the track of moonshine, until they could be seen no longer.

Next morning Jennie was not waiting at the airport for Clive Dumas. He knew, even before the plane touched down, there would be no one there – no one at Fort Colombé either – no one, nothing left. Life for him had become scoured clean, and friendless on that fateful Friday, 13th day of October. Without enthusiasm he gave notice to the police of a missing person. It seemed the thing to do. Then he tried to pick up the fragments of his life and waited for – for what? His sense of failure was immense; and would stay with him for many years. But at least Providence had received Jennie's message and accepted the terms of the bargain. Clive Dumas was safe – miserable, but otherwise unharmed.

Three days after Jennie's disappearance, a woman's body, clad in a white nightdress, was discovered in Crabbey Harbour, gently bumping with the motion of the waves against the hull of Gregory Fain's fishing boat. Clive

Dumas identified the body as that of Mrs Jennie James, late of Bangalore, St Peter Port, Guernsey. The curse of Grand Master de Molay of the Knights Templar, the Poor Knights of Christ and the Temple of Solomon had wreaked its vengeance once more on suffering humanity, whilst serving the cause of the Knights Templar not one jot. And thus another small episode in the fitful history of Templar tradition was closed – or almost so.

Chapter Twenty-One

André walked along the cliff path to the spot where the bungalow called Bangalore once stood. The last year had taken its toll on the old man. Previously, despite his age, his carriage had been erect and his tread firm. Now his shoulders were stooped, his head bowed and his step was slightly hesitant, as though he were unsure of his footing. To catch a fleeting glimpse of him, it might have appeared that he was labouring under a physical burden, but, in reality, all that weighed him down were his thoughts.

For a whole year after the disaster, he had stayed away, unwilling to trigger off bitter memories. But now, on the anniversary of the fire, he seemed drawn back, compelled to return to the place that had for so many years been a second home to him.

But, oh, how things had changed. Even for André, who once knew the garden as well as his own face in the shaving mirror, it was difficult to pick out its features. Once this garden had been more important to him than his own home, but now it was a struggle to imagine what lay beneath the flotsam of vegetation which had been so quickly washed over the site by the mild Guernsey climate. In his imagination he saw the 'new rockery', once planned to be so colourful with heathers and aubretia, never properly completed, now running wild with fern and brambles, and he remembered how he and Jenks had constructed it to conceal the ugly gun-emplacement. With an effort he could still recall where the tidy lawns and rose beds used to be; still smell the sweet mixture of scents from the herb garden; rather less clearly he could imagine the bungalow itself, although André was not one for remembering buildings – only the gardens that surrounded them. Little, though, was left of Bangalore; only an occasional wall, a few feet high, protruded above the scrub of broom and gorse, briar and honeysuckle, which now reigned unchallenged, where once the bungalow had stood. For Bangalore had been wiped almost clean away.

André shook his head in sorrowful disbelief as he wandered amongst his memories of a garden and a building which had once housed people he thought of never quite as friends, but as benevolent employers. And he marvelled that so short a time could have wrought such chaos. Then his thoughts turned to the people – Mrs Grace, Mrs James, both kindly, friendly employers, ladies he was proud to have known. But what of the happenings in this place – happenings they had experienced? Not to mention happenings in the past, maybe the deep and distant past, happenings whose evil had led to this destruction. And what of the emotions such a place had known – the happiness and pain – but the pain particularly, because pain must have far outweighed all other emotions?

As André stood looking at the space that once had contained Bangalore, another man emerged from the bushes and walked towards him. It was a man, André would have preferred not to meet, today or any other day; but one who – just as André – had been compelled by past events and memories to visit the site on that particular day.

They stood at a distance from each other, so as not to intrude on the other's thoughts, as do friends of the deceased at a funeral. André recognised Mrs James's friend from the mainland – the friend who asked too many questions about the German Occupation of Guernsey during the Second World War. For his part, John Frensham recognised Jennie's gardener whom he had believed ignorant and lacking in politeness towards his betters. But today their natural antipathy was subdued by grief. Without complicity, they seemed to agree that quarrels of the past should be shut outside the graveyard's gates – for one day at least. And so they each nodded their recognition simultaneously: no one, thereby, losing face by being the first to give way, or seeming mean-minded by refusing to forgive.

Eventually John Frensham broke the silence. 'I can't get these awful things out of my head,' he said. 'That's why I had to come back, just once, to see if I could make any sense out of it. She was such a nice woman. Did no harm to anyone. Yet these terrible things have happened to her; it makes no sense.'

'I reckon there's no sense in it that anyone could find, no matter how many times they come to gawk at it.' André's voice was uncompromising in its dislike. 'She needed help. And no one *here* could give her that.' The inference was clear – Jennie's mainland friends had failed her, just when she had most needed their support.

'She didn't want my help,' protested John. 'It was offered on more than one occasion – and she declined it. I could tell the way things were going from her letters, but she wouldn't listen to me. She resisted all my efforts to get her away from this place.'

'She didn't want to be away. She thought she belonged here, amongst her folk.' André shook his head again. 'But why she felt that way; God alone knows. She didn't belong – not proper belonging, if you take my meaning. She had no folk here – just memories – and memories can be dangerous things.'

'All that nonsense in her letters about Charles Grace and about the basement...'

'That was no nonsense,' muttered André.

'Moonshine – sheer moonshine! All that stuff about—'

'There was a basement,' André interrupted with some heat. 'Make no mistake about that. There was a basement all right. I saw it with my own eyes. I was there the day Jenks found it. I was the first to set foot in it, come to that – the first since it was closed up anyways. 'Twould have been best if it had stayed closed up, if you ask me. I told Mrs James so at the time. "Best you close it up again and forget about it," I said.'

'Oh come on. How could there have been a basement? Basements don't just appear and disappear when the superstructure burns down. If you're so knowledgeable, just show me where the stair was that led down into it. I've looked all over in this last half hour and I can't find it. There must be a hole in the concrete floor somewhere. But where is it?'

André didn't move. He had no wish to go near that basement. He had more sense than to tempt providence. ''Twas in the corner between the living room and the dining room – beside the great stone fireplace,' he snapped, pointing to what remained of that feature – the one which John had admired so much, during his convalescence at Bangalore, now just a shoulder-high lump of masonry and tumbled stone, projecting through the debris.

'And where is it now?' John persisted.

André gave a shrug of his shoulders and turned away. 'The basement *was* there. I saw it. I stood in it.'

John followed André's retreating back, catching the few pearls that he scattered tantalisingly in his wake.

'Some young fellow got hisself trapped down there t'other day and had to be rescued. Some young chap off Alderney, so the story goes. After that, they got a bulldozer in and pushed all the rubble into the hole to fill it in. Less dangerous that way – for kids and the like.'

'And what do you know about Charles Grace?' John insisted.

André halted and turned a sullen face towards him. 'As far as Mr Grace goes; no one ever knew the truth about him.'

'Come on and have a beer with me,' suggested John. 'We ought to talk.'

André hesitated for an instant, then he suddenly seemed to decide that it could do no harm to talk to this mainlander, despite his natural antipathy. He still, however, could not acknowledge in words the olive branch which John had extended. He merely nodded his agreement.

In the Harbour Bar, the one where Jennie and Clive had had their rendezvous, the atmosphere between the two men relaxed under the influence of Guernsey Best Bitter. Before long, confidences began to be exchanged.

John spoke first: 'Jennie – Mrs James, that is – seemed to have some crazy notion that Charles Grace's spirit still lived at Bangalore. She wrote me letters – many letters, telling me all sorts of cock-and-bull stories about Charles Grace – that he had led her to the basement and was protecting her from some evil influence in the place. All manner of rubbish like that. Latterly, though, she seemed to think something had changed – that his presence had become more threatening, but I couldn't make any sense out of what she was trying to tell me. Towards the end she seemed scared out of her wits about something, or someone – maybe him, maybe someone, or something else. I just don't know. Reading those letters made me fear for her state of mind; and after the dreadful business of her death, one really can't help wondering. Was it an accident, or suicide maybe?'

'They said it were an accident. That's good enough for me.' André's face had assumed a particularly stubborn expression, as he stared into his beer. He was silent for a long time. Then he started speaking, slowly and deliberately, and so quietly that John had to lean across the table towards him to catch his words: 'I saw Charles Grace – after the war, I mean when he wasn't supposed to be on the island at all. A lot of folks said he never came back to Guernsey after the war, but I know he did. He was at Bangalore, whatever they might say.' André took a long drink from his pint pot. John waited, feeling there was more to come. André's eyes ranged round the bar, not looking at John. At last he spoke again, 'He never talked to me, though – never came up close, like. It was as though he didn't want to be seen, although he was kind of careless with me and I used to catch sight of him times without number – out of the corner of my eyes, as you might say – while I was working in the garden. I heard Mrs Grace talking to him too – but I never heard his voice. "What do you think about this, Charles?" she would say. "Oh yes, I do agree with you. Over here, don't you think? Absolutely right, Charles." All that sort of thing went on, all the time. Charles Grace was there all right. Same as he was there with Mrs James – towards the end. I swear to it. Although I'd never breathe a word to anyone what wasn't a real close friend of hers.'

'Do you really mean what you're saying?' exclaimed John. 'Even though everyone says he'd been dead for years.'

'He was there all right. Reckon he always was, and always will be, most like,' said André mysteriously; and then, as though he had already said too much, he swilled down his beer and left the bar without uttering another word, merely nodding a sullen thank you towards the mainlander as he went.

John remained behind, finishing his beer and mulling over André's words. Little did he know that he was sitting at the same table Jennie had occupied with Clive Dumas the day they talked about the destruction of the Knights

Templar. He looked out of the window, seeing the view they had seen: the harbour full of deserted yachts, waiting for their owners to tear themselves away from their centrally heated winter homes and beguiling suntan lamps; the quarrelsome seagulls, skirling in an endless bad-tempered ballet; the dark castle brooding over the harbour entrance. All this John watched for a long time. Then, as the light started to fade, he rose and left the bar.

Slowly he walked up the winding streets in the gathering dusk back to the desolation which was all that remained of Bangalore. He stood once more – for one last time, he was sure – on the concrete ground floor, picturing in his mind the house in which he had spent that troubled convalescence after his heart attack. He traced the walls between the kitchen and the dining room, between the dining room and the lounge and there, over one of Jennie's missing corners stood a huge pile of rubble. Covering the blasted stairwell, I suppose, he thought.

In the other wing of the bungalow, John stood in what had been, for a short time, his bedroom during his stay at Bangalore – a room in which he had lain so many nights and pictured Jennie, the woman he had hoped one day to be able to cherish, sleeping in the next room in Mrs Grace's 'dear bed'.

Then, with a shock, he realised that the huge metal frame of her bed had survived the fire. It still stood in what used to be Jennie's room – a poor relic of its past magnificence. Its carved head and foot boards had disappeared in the fire, only the frame remained, drunkenly supported on the charred remnants of the massive, carved mahogany legs. John ran his hands over the rough and filthy metalwork, thinking of Jennie and wishing things had been different between them when they had met for the last time – even wishing (despite the imposition of Clive Dumas) that he had had the chance to see her just once during her final trip to London.

'Too late; it's all too late. Why does life always boil down to the expression "if-only"?' he muttered.

Perched precariously on the bed frame, John fell into a daydream, in which his mind flipped through a rapid replay of all those parts of his life that had been touched by Jennie; and as he did so, his fingers idly caressed the nearest leg of the bedstead. Suddenly, under his hand, the leg changed shape. Immediately all his senses sprang alive, concentrating on the wood beneath his fingers. It seemed as though a small piece of the carving had sprung aside, like a tiny secret panel, to reveal a hollowed-out cavity within the leg. His fingers explored this cavity. There was something loose, lying within. He withdrew it and found it was nothing but a fragment of charred wood. This he was about to throw away, when something made him pause and, holding it up to his eyes in the fading light, he examined it more closely. There was something unusual about its texture. It didn't feel like wood; and indeed, the more he examined it, the more sure he became that it was a tiny piece of charred bone. Not a fragment even. It was a whole bone; but one so tiny, it must have come from a limb no bigger than a finger, or a toe. John was no expert in anatomy and could not even tell if the bone was human or came from some animal. Of only one thing he was sure: that as he held it in his hand, he became conscious of an unfamiliar prickling sensation. It started at the tips of his fingers holding the bone, spread rapidly throughout his hand, up his forearm, through his elbow and up to his shoulder. As he peered at the bone, the prickling became an ache, the ache became an excruciating pain, which crept up his neck and settled blindly behind his eyes. Leaping up from the bed, he threw the bone from him with all the force he could muster. Instantly the pain ceased and he stood watching as the bone skimmed the ground, seeming to gather momentum as it went.

Up and up it sped, through the trees that lined the cliff top and out over the sea. And now it seemed to be glowing. How else would he have been able to see such a tiny object in the gathering dusk? And then, for no apparent reason, it changed direction and dived out of sight towards the breakers at the foot of the cliff.

Even as he stood, wondering at what he had just seen (or thought he had seen) John became aware of two figures walking in the dusk under the trees. The woman had an unmistakable poise and agile step, that he could not fail to recognise from long, long ago. She had the bearing and carriage of the young girl, whom he had watched with envy on the day when she had married his best friend. Now, practically thirty years later, she was here again, walking with the sprightliness of youth along the cliff path. But now she was not walking with Greg, but with another man – a man, John instinctively knew was Charles Grace. They moved like lovers, ageless and sensual. They passed into the shadows and suddenly they were gone. The place was deserted. John was alone, standing in the ruins of Bangalore, that eccentric dream house which once had belonged to the girl he would always remember – the girl he would always love. And at last a great weight was lifted from his soul. John Frensham was a free man once more.

As he left the ruins of Jennie's idiosyncratic house, John Frensham pondered over his fleeting impression of Charles Grace. All he had been able to see of him in the poor light was a shape and a movement – the hunch of his shoulders, the inclination of his head, his loose-limbed stride – yet all these were unmistakably familiar. 'I wonder if Jennie ever realised,' he mused, 'how much Charles Grace resembles Greg.'

Epilogue

It remains an open question whether John Frensham's method of disposing of the relic met Le Messurier's criteria. After all, throwing the irritating object over the cliff could hardly be described as a burial 'with due respect'; although apparently it was the only burial accorded to Charles Grace himself, if Jennie's dream is to be believed.

All that is certain is that, within the year, John Frensham suffered another and, this time, fatal heart attack. It could be argued that this was only to be expected, after the warning he had received two years before. Alternatively, John Frensham, too, might have become an unintentional transgressor, and therefore vulnerable to de Molay's curse – the latest in a long line of men and women to be 'summoned before the throne of God to account for their actions against the Knights Templar'.

If the contemporary records are to be believed (and they cannot be guaranteed to be one hundred per cent reliable), there were no temporal or geographical limitations set in the old man's call for vengeance. The assumption, therefore, must be that the effects of his wrath will continue for as long as there is one remaining Templar relic extant; and innocent transgressors, like Jennie James and John Frensham, who simply stumble into a web of intrigue, woven centuries before, will pay the price.

There still exists an empty plot of land on the cliff top to the south of St Peter Port, a curiously idiosyncratic neighbour to the villas of the rich and famous which now line that particular road. For Guernsey today is a very different place from the Guernsey of the decades immediately after the Second World War. But it still remains an island of legend and mystery, and a strong belief survives there in the chilling presence of the dead and the unearthly command of medieval curses.